RUSTLER'S VENOM

Also by W.W. Lee
Rogue's Gold

RUSTLER'S VENOM

W.W. Lee

Walker and Company
New York

First published in the United States of America in 1990
by Walker Publishing Company, Inc.

Published simultaneously in Canada by Thomas Allen & Son
Canada, Limited, Markham, Ontario

Library of Congress Cataloging-in-Publication Data

Lee, W. W. (Wendi W.)
Rustler's venom / W.W. Lee.
ISBN 0-8027-4112-6
I. Title.
PS3562.E3663R87   1990
813'.54—dc20   90-35468
CIP

Printed in the United States of America

2 4 6 8 10 9 7 5 3 1

For Grandma Weberg
With love

ACKNOWLEDGMENTS

THANKS are due to the following people for their support: my husband, Terry Beatty, for his encouragement and Max Allan Collins, for his time and generosity. Thanks also go to Barbara Peuchner and Jackie Johnson.

CHAPTER 1

MATTIE'S hands felt raw from stringing snake wire between fence posts. Early that morning, she'd announced to her ranch hands that she'd be riding fences with Omaha. He'd replied, "Oh, Mrs. Quinn. You don't really want to do that."

She pulled her hat off, shook her dark hair loose, and said, "Yes, I do, Omaha. I have to learn how to make repairs just like the rest of you now that I'm running the ranch."

Mattie had deliberately chosen to ride fences that morning so she could work with Omaha. She'd pulled on her late husband Joe's old work clothes, which were so big that Mattie had to roll up the pants and sleeves and cut another hole in his belt to secure the waist around her trim figure.

Of her three remaining ranch hands, John "Omaha" Johanson was the hired hand with whom she felt most comfortable. A tall, fair-haired man with a ruddy outdoors complexion, Omaha was the least judgmental of Mattie's determination to run the ranch since Joe was laid in the ground.

Charley Stacks, the ranch foreman, had been with the Quinns since they started the ranch five years ago. He was a man of average height and weight, graying on the sides and thinning on top. Mattie couldn't recall ever seeing him crack a smile. His features seemed to be fixed in a permanently disagreeable expression. Sometimes when Mattie turned away from Charley, she could feel his disapproving stare and could almost hear him saying, "A woman shouldn't ought to be running a ranch—even if she *is* a widow."

Slim, on the other hand, seemed to have a smile pasted on his face all the time. He was just under six feet tall with a

1

slight paunch. Even under the deep lines carved out by outdoor living, Slim still had baby-faced features.

Mattie couldn't recall Slim's real name, although when he'd hired on six months ago he'd given it readily enough. It was a long, foreign-sounding name and the hands just got tired of trying to pronounce it, so they started calling him Slim. It stuck and now no one could remember his Christian name. Maybe even Slim would have a hard time recalling it.

Although Mattie sometimes worked with Slim—and never with Charley—there was something about Slim beneath his constant smile that made Mattie a little uncomfortable. She had to admit that she couldn't put her finger on what it was. He never said anything out of line when he was around her, never displayed any discourtesy toward his female employer, but Mattie made sure she didn't work around Slim any more than she had to.

Ever since Joe Quinn was killed four months ago, Mattie had been determined to keep the cattle business going. There were several prominent cattle ranchers around who may have put a little pressure on Marshal Cobb to declare Joe's death an accident, but Mattie knew in her bones that her husband had been killed in cold blood.

A few weeks before his death, there had been two offers to buy their ranch: one came from Amos Blackiston and another came from Luther Capwell. It wasn't surprising that both cattle kings wanted to own the Quinn property. Although it wasn't more than thirty-five acres, Joe Quinn had chosen his land well. Rattler Creek, a tributary of the Powder River, ran from the northwest corner of the Quinn property down through Amos Blackiston's property, eventually running into Wyoming Territory. It was renamed Clear Fork down there.

Both Blackiston and Capwell were well known in the town of Rattlesnake and the surrounding southeast corner of the Montana Territory. They ran the Montana Cattlemen's Association, a group of ranchers who owned large cattle spreads in the county. Joe used to tell Mattie that the only requirements for joining were an insatiable greed and the ability to covet your neighbor's land.

Mattie remembered the day Blackiston came to try to buy out Joe. She was fetching two glasses of whiskey for the men, and when she entered the study her husband was sitting at his desk, listening with a stony face to what Amos Blackiston had come to discuss.

Mattie's heart raced when she caught sight of her husband from across a room. He was still a good-looking man despite the years of hardship they'd had to endure when they moved out to the Montana Territory. He had sharply handsome features that were softened by warm brown eyes and a ready smile. When his shock of auburn hair grew too long, he would tie it back with a cloth or leather strip until he found the time to get it cut.

The sight of Amos Blackiston sitting across from Joe brought an overwhelming rush of anger and revulsion to Mattie. Blackiston was fat and had a stubby little porcine nose. Mattie pitied Mrs. Blackiston for having to live with a man who so resembled a pig. His mannerisms and movements were equally swinelike.

Amos Blackiston was a greedy man who had driven several small cattle ranchers out of the area; he felt he needed more land to add to an already excessive cattle empire. Some of the ranchers had gladly taken Blackiston's generous property settlement and moved on, but the men who got in Blackiston's way were ruined for life.

Most of the ex-ranchers who were forced out had moved away and tried to piece their lives together elsewhere, but Mattie remembered that at least one old man was still living in Rattlesnake. He was too old to build another ranch. Instead, he took work at the stables and began to spend his "generous property settlement" on drink to forget the bitter memories of what Amos Blackiston had done to him.

"Look, Quinn," he said bluntly. "I need your land. I'm

buying more cattle and expanding. I'll pay good money for the land. I want to be the biggest cattle rancher in this territory."

Joe was shaking his head. "I can't sell you my land, Amos. Me and Mattie worked hard for it. When we start a family, we want a place for our children to grow up."

Blackiston leaned forward. "I can get you some real nice property to start over. The northwest corner of my land. Lots of trees . . ."

"Lots of places for cattle to wander," Joe said drily, "like Powder Ridge. And there's no water. No, thank you. We don't aim to move."

Later that day Joe turned Luther Capwell down also. Although Capwell didn't own as much land as Blackiston, he had much more influence in the county. While Blackiston mindlessly acquired land as if it were the only thing saving him from poverty, Capwell invested in land like he might invest in a bank. Luther Capwell was a handsome man with a bushy mustache and black slicked-back hair. He dressed like a gambler with brocade vests, starched linen shirts, and fancy boots.

It was rumored that Luther Capwell came from a wealthy family and had gotten a debutante in the family way, then refused to marry her. Despite this story, which Capwell neither confirmed nor denied, people in Rattlesnake liked him. Oh, there were whispers that he was behind some of the trouble on the smaller ranches. But there wasn't anything to go on aside from the gossip.

The next day, things started to go wrong around the Quinn ranch. First, it was discovered that all the fences on the northern boundary of the Quinn property were torn up. Joe didn't connect it with Blackiston and Capwell immediately, but several days after repairing the fences, fifty head of Quinn cattle disappeared.

Blackiston made another offer to buy the Quinn land—this time for a lower price. That's when Joe made the connection between the misfortune he'd been having around the ranch lately and his rejection of the offers to sell his land. That night at supper, he told Mattie of his suspicions.

When he finished, Mattie asked, "Which one do you think is behind the torn fences and stolen cattle?"

Her husband shrugged. "Amos Blackiston is my guess. Our property lines meet and he's not happy about sharing Rattler Creek with us."

Mattie asked, "What about Luther Capwell? He might do something like this if he wanted it bad enough."

Joe rubbed his neck and looked thoughtful. "It might be Luther, but with Amos, it makes more sense, don't it?"

Mattie tried to understand. "Why does he want our property so badly? Why does Blackiston need to own all the land that Rattler Creek runs through?"

Joe put his hand over hers and said, "Well, honey, there's just some greedy sons of bitches out there and Amos Blackiston is the worst of them." He took a deep breath. His face looked weary from a hard day's work and he shook his head as if to wake up. "For Amos, I think he's gotten it into his head that someday I'll dam up the river and he won't be able to water his cattle."

His wife exclaimed, "That's preposterous! You told him you'd never do a thing like that, didn't you?"

"Of course. Why would I do a damn fool thing like that? There's plenty of water for everyone. But Amos is dishonest so he just assumes everyone else is, too."

Mattie got to thinking about their problem again. Reaching across the table to touch her husband's forearm lightly, she said, "Is there any reason Luther Capwell might be doing this? Our water doesn't run through his property; why would he want it?"

Joe had to think about it for a minute. If there was a reason, it was very subtle or was something the Quinns hadn't discovered for themselves yet. He finally shook his head. "It's probably just a good business move on his part. He's the one who started the Association and he would just want to add this land to what he already owns. Besides, he might've heard that Amos made a bid on it. They've always competed—who has the most land, the most cattle, the best stock."

"Whoever's doing this won't leave us alone, will he?" Mattie said. "What are we going to do?"

Joe passed his free hand over his face, stopping to rub the bridge of his nose briefly. "I've been putting this off, but it looks like I'll have to ride into Rattlesnake tomorrow and have a talk with Marshal Cobb. Maybe he'll find out who did it and put a stop to it."

Mattie didn't have to voice her misgivings. She knew why Joe hadn't been to Gordy Cobb yet. Cobb appeared to be a good lawman, having kept the peace in Rattlesnake for the five years Joe and Mattie Quinn had lived in the area. But lately there had been rumors that Marshal Cobb was being paid a little extra by the Association to keep watch over their properties.

Cobb had paid a price for accepting the cattle barons' money: he'd lost the trust of the Rattlesnake citizens. Anytime a citizen had any trouble with Amos Blackiston, no one bothered to tell the marshal about it.

More likely, the citizen with the complaint just ended up giving in to Blackiston's bullying tactics. Although no complaint had ever been formally lodged against Luther Capwell, it was not a secret that Capwell was one of the first buyers on an abandoned piece of property.

A few months before Joe's death, Casper James just packed up and moved out one night. It wasn't the first time a man had given up on a perfectly good piece of land around Rattlesnake, but Casper had been doing well as a cattle rancher. Luther Capwell was there immediately to claim the James land. There were a few rumors that Capwell or Blackiston had "encouraged" James to leave, but no one could ever prove anything. And Casper James wasn't around anymore to tell his side of the story.

The night Joe told her his suspicions and his plans to see Marshal Cobb was the last time Mattie saw Joe alive. Right after supper, he went outside to clean his Winchester. While Mattie was cleaning up the kitchen, she heard the sound of a horse approaching. Since they rarely had visitors, Mattie set aside her work to peek out the front window.

Joe was sitting on a tree stump in the clearing, his rifle resting against his knee and the oil-covered patch on the end of the cleaning rod drooping from his hand as if he'd paused in the midst of cleaning the barrel. He was looking up in the distance, his ear cocked as if he were straining to hear some faraway sound.

After a few minutes no one rode up, so Mattie shook her head and went back to the kitchen. She was beginning to wonder if she'd imagined the sound of a horse when she heard Joe's voice shouting, followed by the sound of a gunshot.

Mattie dropped the metal pot she had been cleaning and ran outside. All was quiet, except for the distant thrum of hooves. Joe lay crumpled on the ground in a pool of blood, the rifle at his side.

The ranch hands ran up from the bunkhouse, their guns cocked and ready, but too late. Mattie was bent over his body, too stunned for tears. Without knowing why, she reached out and touched Joe's rifle before one of the men pulled her away from the gruesome scene. The barrel was cool to her touch.

The rest of that night was a red haze for the new widow. She vaguely remembered Slim and Charley riding out to get the marshal and a doctor from the nearby town of Rattlesnake. It seemed to take forever for them to return. Marshal Cobb prowled around the clearing and asked a few questions. Mattie numbly recounted the order of events to him. The doctor pronounced Joe dead, then gave Mattie a sleeping powder and sent her off to bed.

When the marshal returned the next day to pay his respects, he told Mattie that he was finished investigating Joe's death. He called it an accident. From all indications, a round had been left in the rifle chamber and had gone off when Joe was cleaning the inside of the barrel. Mattie tried to recall the scene when she found Joe, but it was fuzzy in her mind now.

She told Marshal Cobb about the offers from Blackiston and Capwell. She couldn't remember her answers to his questions from the night before, so she decided to go through her story again.

Gordy Cobb shifted uncomfortably and said in a hesitant voice, "You don't have to do this, ma'am. You told me what you saw and what you did last night."

Mattie was certain that if she went through her story again, Marshal Cobb would see that Joe's death wasn't just an accident. "But what about the horse I heard?"

"What horse?"

"Like I told you last night. I heard a horse just before Joe was shot!"

"But did you see it? Was there a rider?"

She sighed. "No. I looked out the front window and all I saw was Joe sitting there with his Winchester. He had stopped cleaning it and was looking off in the distance, like he'd heard it, too."

Marshal Cobb frowned.

Mattie added, "After the shot, I ran out to find Joe lying there. I know I heard the sound of someone riding away."

Cobb was silent for a moment as if he were trying to sort it all out. Finally, he said, "Well, Mrs. Quinn, after a shock like this, it's hard for anyone to recall exactly what happened. I've heard people tell a story three or more times, and each time something new crops up in the telling." Cobb was quick to add, "Not that you're lying. I'm sure right now you think you heard that horse."

Mattie opened her mouth to protest. She was furious that Cobb would infer that she wasn't telling the truth.

But the marshal cut her off before she could say anything. "Please don't be angry with me. It's just that I've seen a lot of death and grief in my time. I know you think you heard that horse. Living out here can play tricks on your hearing. You can hear something that sounds nearby but it's a mile away."

"No, Marshal," she started to say, "that couldn't be . . ."

He patted her shoulder awkwardly as if he weren't listening to her and said, "He probably didn't even come near your place. That probably explains it."

He had dismissed it without even giving her testimony serious consideration. But Mattie knew that from the kitchen, which was situated in the back, the sound of a horse approaching would sound very faint unless the rider came straight up to the house. That theory Cobb had spouted about being able to hear a horse going by a mile away was utter nonsense.

Mattie contained her growing fury at the marshal's stubborn refusal to consider further investigation. She tried another tactic. "Joe was too careful to leave a cartridge in his rifle while he cleaned it."

"Now, just a minute, Mrs. Quinn," the marshal replied, holding up his hand. "Are you suggesting that it was murder? I know how you must feel with Joe gone. His death was senseless." Marshal Cobb shook his head sympathetically. "But you mustn't start getting fanciful ideas. Empty accusations could stir up a whole lot of trouble here in Rattlesnake County, for no good reason."

Just before he mounted his horse, Gordy Cobb turned back to her and said, "I suppose you'll be wanting to sell this place now, Mrs. Quinn. I'm sure you'll fetch a good price for it. You have some of the best water rights around, you know."

With that, he tipped his hat to her and rode away.

Mattie stamped her foot in frustration. Somehow, she had to find out who killed her husband, but she didn't know where to turn.

Slim addressed her. "I'll ride Scrapper today, Mrs. Quinn."

Scrapper had been Joe's favorite horse.

Mattie replied absently, "Leave him in the pasture today, Slim."

"But ma'am," Slim argued, "Scrapper needs exercise and I thought . . ."

"I said no," Mattie snapped. She watched Slim back away warily, hat in hand. He was right—Scrapper needed exercise. But she'd be the one to ride her husband's horse.

If Charley weren't already foreman of the Quinn ranch, she'd have given Omaha the job. Mattie was grateful for the patience and respect he'd shown her when she'd decided to keep the ranch and work beside the ranch hands.

Young widows out west rarely stayed and ran their husband's property. Most of them, while still in mourning, would sell their late husband's property and possessions and hop a stagecoach heading back east to their families.

Of course, if Joe hadn't died so suddenly a few months ago, she'd still be happily keeping house instead of riding fences. The doubt and anger flared up in her again. Mattie had to keep a tight rein on her emotions these days, what with the suspicion she had that the Cattlemen's Association had something to do with Joe's death.

She addressed her companion. "That's all for today, Omaha. The other boys ought to be back from Rattlesnake by now and supper isn't far off."

Omaha nodded, touched his hat, and said, "Yes, ma'am. We sure worked up an appetite today."

They rode back toward the ranch. Omaha would head for the bunkhouse to get cleaned up while Mattie would go to the kitchen to start the meal. These days, Mattie didn't have time to fix more than one hearty meal a day. In the morning, the hands fixed their own breakfasts, and packed a few things for a midafternoon break out on the range.

As it was, Mattie had other worries. She needed a few more hands now that the time to move cattle was coming up soon.

But she shrugged off the urgency again as they approached the ranch.

Omaha noted the absence of the wagon. "Charley and Slim ain't back from Rattlesnake yet."

But Mattie wasn't concerned about the absence of the wagon. She stood frozen in horror, staring beyond the clearing to the front door.

Old Gumption, Joe's prize bull, had been slaughtered and left in front of the house. Mutilated was a more accurate word. Some of Old Gumption's blood had been used to write the words "Get Out Or Die!" on the door.

The bull had been raised by Joe; for a moment, she felt sadness overwhelm her. Then she took a deep breath and got angry, so angry that she was shaking. She wouldn't be pushed out of her home—not after Joe died for taking a stand.

Her voice sounded unnaturally loud in the face of such silent carnage. "When Charley and Slim return from town, you'd better drag what's left of Old Gumption out to the smokehouse. Can't afford to waste all that meat."

"I can start without them, Mrs. Quinn," Omaha replied, his voice tight with anger. Mattie looked at Omaha's stony face. It was hard to tell what he was thinking.

He caught sight of her pensive look and his face softened. "I'm sorry, Mrs. Quinn," he said. "I'm just wishing I could catch the bastard who did this. Joe was so proud of Old Gumption."

Mattie sighed wearily. "I know. You'd better get started. We don't want the meat to spoil."

He wheeled his horse around and headed for the smokehouse to get a wagon and some hooks.

Mattie felt a tear slip down her cheek and she struggled for control. She had to keep up a strong front, show her hands that she wasn't afraid. For a moment, she entertained the idea of going to Marshal Cobb, but soon waved that notion aside.

I need help from outside Rattlesnake, Mattie thought. Last night while she was going through Joe's desk, she had come across an advertisement clipped from a newspaper. The advertisement read: *Tisdale Investigations—Confidential Detective Agency. All manner of problems solved and mysteries uncovered. Our trained investigators are discreet and thorough. Contact Arthur Tisdale, General Delivery, San Francisco, California.*

She couldn't imagine why Joe had kept it without telling her, but after supper tonight she was determined to sit down at the desk and write to one Mr. Arthur Tisdale.

CHAPTER 2

JEFFERSON Birch could see Arthur Tisdale's arrival from the saloon across the street. A cloud of dust accompanied the stagecoach's approach. It had been almost a year since he met Tisdale for the first time and it had been a short meeting. Birch hoped he'd still recognize his employer, but since a stagecoach held only about six passengers, he didn't think it would be difficult to pick Arthur Tisdale out of the crowd.

Running his hand over his light brown hair, Birch squinted his gray eyes, watching with amusement as a short, natty figure emerged from the carriage, still swaying slightly from the continuous side-to-side movement of the trip. While the man had the bearing of Arthur Tisdale, an absurd walrus mustache threatened to engulf him at any moment. Birch shook his head and finished his whiskey, then started on the beer chaser. He looked back at the stagecoach, expecting to see Tisdale at any moment, but all he saw was the small, well-dressed man with the giant waxed mustache.

Birch peered at the man across the street. It couldn't be Tisdale, Birch thought to himself, could it? Birch tried to recall that afternoon almost a year ago when he met Arthur Tisdale at that Jacksonville hotel in the Oregon Territory.

For the life of him, Birch couldn't figure out why Tisdale had chosen to meet in the town of Rosebud. It was situated on a tributary of the Yellowstone River in the middle of Montana Territory. There were only a few other small towns nearby, and those were mostly built up from former army foundations such as Old Fort Alexander and Fort C.P. Smith. While the western half of the territory had established towns around gold and copper mining, the eastern half consisted mostly of grassland with occasional patches of scrub, cedar, and pine.

With a sigh, Birch decided that the dapper gent must be Arthur Tisdale. The man was pacing back and forth, like an impatient rooster, in front of the stagecoach. He checked his pocket watch every few minutes, scrutinizing every man who matched Birch's general description.

Birch grabbed his hat and jammed it on his head. Finishing his beer, he glanced briefly in the mirror behind the bar. His own sun-weathered, strong-jawed face stared back. With a finger, Birch raised the brim a bit, adjusted his gunbelt, and left the saloon.

The natty little man's face brightened as Birch walked toward him. "So good of you to meet me here, Mr. Birch," Arthur Tisdale greeted him. He stroked his mustache slowly.

Birch said, "It took me a moment to recognize you, Mr. Tisdale. You didn't have that mustache when we first met."

Tisdale puffed up, a pleased look on his face. "It really makes me look more dashing, doesn't it?"

"Well, dashing isn't quite the word I had in mind," Birch said carelessly. Tisdale looked mildly inquisitive. "What I mean to say is," Birch said hastily, "that it's not quite the word I was looking for, but now that you've mentioned it, dashing it is."

Birch stared at it for a second or two longer, then added, "What's our first order of business, Mr. Tisdale?"

Arthur Tisdale looked down at his bag and said, "I really should check into a hotel."

"Well, there's only one place here in town." Birch gestured to the saloon across the street, the very one he'd just had a drink in. "They rent rooms above the saloon. It's not fancy, but they do provide a bed and a hearty breakfast."

Tisdale looked at the Steer and Saddle Saloon in dismay, then shrugged. "Ah, well. I shouldn't expect much out in this godforsaken territory. I'll be on the stagecoach back to the state of California tomorrow. Shall we?"

The bartender, a short, burly fellow, doubled as desk clerk. With Tisdale's room paid for and his carpet bag safely ensconced in a modest room above the Steer and Saddle Saloon, Birch and Tisdale settled downstairs at a table with a bottle of bourbon between them.

Birch had been a Texas Ranger for over five years, spending most of his time tracking rustlers, robbers, and murderers. His last assignment had been tracking horse thieves across the Rio Grande. It was supposed to be an easy job that would get him home in time to be with Audrey during the birth of their first child. Instead, it had taken almost a week of negotiations with the Mexican Army to retrieve the rustlers. By the time he'd returned home, his wife and baby had been laid to rest.

Audrey had died during childbirth, and the baby, a boy, had been a sickly thing who hadn't lived more than an hour outside the womb. Birch turned in his Ranger badge and traveled west, picking up work wherever he could find it.

He was working on a ranch outside of Stockton when he read Arthur Tisdale's advertisement in the local newspaper: "Looking for a man who welcomes adventure, a man who has keen insight and investigative experience. Send reply care of General Delivery, San Francisco."

Birch wasn't sure what the job entailed exactly, but he interpreted "adventure" as danger and sent an inquiry to Tisdale the very same day. Several days later, he received a reply from Tisdale requesting a meeting up in Jacksonville in Oregon Territory. Birch collected his wages from the ranch owner and headed north, not knowing what to expect.

Nearly a year had passed since he had signed on as a freelance investigator for Tisdale Investigations. As his first assignment, he'd broken up a gang of road agents terrorizing the citizens of Grant's Pass, a gold-mining community. Since that time, Birch had taken on odd jobs, working his way across Oregon Territory, through Idaho and Wyoming, all the while keeping Tisdale informed of his whereabouts. A few days ago, Birch received an urgent telegram from Arthur Tisdale to meet him in Rosebud, Montana, in a week's time.

Again, Birch collected wages owed him from a ranch owner and .headed north. He arrived in Rosebud a day before Tisdale and spent the time observing the townsfolk, drinking whiskey, and looking for women who resembled his late wife Audrey. There were times when this obsessive pastime brought him great pleasure, when a memory would come flooding in as thick and sweet as honey on bread. Other times, the memory was more bitter than sweet.

He seemed to find at least one Audrey lookalike in every town. Sometimes he felt a twinge when he passed a young woman who smiled a particular way, reminding Birch of the seventeen-year-old Audrey whom he courted. At other times, he would ache when he caught sight of an older version of Audrey, the woman she might have become if she'd lived. But he felt an unbearable pain when he walked past a young mother with her son. Those were the times he would turn into the nearest saloon and order a bottle of whiskey and a glass, sit in a far corner, and toss down drink after drink silently.

Birch hadn't seen anyone yet who resembled Audrey here in Rosebud. He straddled a fence between disappointment and relief. But now was not the time to think about his late wife. Birch sat across the table from Arthur Tisdale, two glasses of bourbon placed on the table between them.

Tisdale took a delicate sip from his glass before beginning. "I apologize for the delay in getting you another assignment. It takes time to get an agency going."

Birch shrugged. He really hadn't expected to hear from Tisdale again and didn't consider himself a permanent employee of Tisdale Investigations. But he had to ask himself why he left his job in Wyoming when Tisdale's telegram arrived. He wasn't sure he had an answer.

Tisdale cleared his throat. "I have been in contact with a woman named Mattie Quinn. She lives just outside of Rattlesnake, Montana, near Powder River." He pulled out a neatly folded letter and a pair of spectacles from a coat pocket. After securing the eyeglass wires behind his ears, he consulted the letter, holding it at arm's length and squinting a bit. "She needs someone who could help her out of a difficult situation. Apparently, Mrs. Quinn is a recent widow and is having trouble with the local Cattlemen's Association."

"Does that mean she owns a ranch?"

Arthur Tisdale looked up at Birch and nodded. "Yes, I believe she inherited her husband's ranch when he died of an accident . . ." Here Tisdale paused, scrutinizing the letter, then continued. "But she doesn't believe it *was* an accident."

"I suppose this is a job that requires me to be there immediately."

Tisdale put his eyeglasses away, then surprised Birch by drinking the rest of his bourbon in one long gulp. "I imagine you're right," the man in the neat suit said as he smoothed his mustache. "By the way, you do still have the badge I gave you for identification, don't you?"

Birch wasn't sure where he'd put it, but he could probably lay his hands on it if asked to produce the tin star. "It's in a safe place," he reassured his employer.

Tisdale nodded, apparently satisfied that his tin badge would be the answer to any problem Birch might encounter. Reaching into his vest pocket, Tisdale extracted a paper and handed it to Birch. "You might want to keep this with you." It was Mattie Quinn's letter to Arthur Tisdale.

The head of the investigation agency suggested that they get some dinner.

Birch left that afternoon, not even waiting to get an early start the next morning. Tisdale had little else to offer Birch in the way of information, but urged his agent to be careful on his journey to Rattlesnake.

Birch rode all night and into the next day, stopping only to rest his horse, Cactus, and to get water from the streams and creeks that ran off from the Yellowstone River.

Huge gray clouds were rolling across the Montana sky on the afternoon that he arrived in Rattlesnake. It was a dusty little town with only one saloon. Most towns with a population of little more than one hundred had a room built in the back of a general supply store, especially for locking up the drunk who shot up the saloon on Saturday night. But Birch noted that Rattlesnake had a marshal's office and a jail in the back.

Birch dismounted in front of a weathered building with no sign to indicate that it was a saloon. But from the drunks who staggered out the batwing doors, Birch knew this was where he could get a drink and some information.

The inside was as faded as the outside. There were a few dusty tables and chairs scattered around. A blowsy saloon gal sat with a customer at a table near the bar. Her hand rested on the man's leg as they talked in low tones to each other.

The bartender watched warily as Birch approached the bar.

"Whiskey." Birch laid a coin out on the bar. Greed replaced the uneasy look in the barkeep's eye as he swept the money into his pocket, poured out a measure and set it in front of Birch.

He asked cheerfully, "Just passing through?"

Birch downed his drink, paid for another shot, and replied, "Actually, I'm looking for the Quinn place."

The bartender looked up sharply from pouring, then set the generous measure of liquor down. "Why do you want to go there for? The widow Quinn should be selling her place any day now."

Birch squinted at the wary barkeep and raised his eyebrows. "Oh? That's not what I heard."

"You some kind of gunslinger looking for work?" the

bartender asked. " 'Cause if you are, I can tell you right now that there's no place for you here. Marshal Cobb will set you straight if you don't take my warning and clear out after you finish that drink."

Birch replied mildly, "I'm not a hired gun. I'm looking for ranch work. Last place I worked was down in Wyoming. The owner didn't need me anymore, so I moved on. I heard the Quinn place could use another hand."

The bartender's suspicious expression melted away. In a gruff voice, he said, "You want to hire onto a ranch, stranger? Take my advice and stay away from Mattie Quinn. She's just trouble. Now if you want work, mister, why don't you go see Luther Capwell or Amos Blackiston. They got big ranches and are always looking for a good hand."

Birch thought it was better to not argue with this man so he said, "Give me directions to all three, then."

They stepped outside so the bartender could show Birch how to get to Blackiston's ranch. A black plume of smoke rose from the east.

"By God," the bartender yelled, "I think that smoke's coming from the Quinn place."

Birch jumped on Cactus and headed toward the smoke at a full gallop.

CHAPTER 3

"GET the bucket out of the kitchen, Charley!" Mattie kept an eye on the barn while she barked out her instructions. "There's another one around the side of the house, too."

Slim called out, "What should I do, Mrs. Quinn?"

She hesitated, unsure of what else needed to be done—there had never been a fire on the ranch before. She felt her stomach tighten as if she were going to throw up. The horses suddenly flashed into her mind. Why hadn't she immediately thought of them? Were the horses safe or were they still in the burning barn? She didn't hear frantic, panicking whinnies coming from the collapsing structure, but she thought it would be best to check on their whereabouts.

The wind shifted and thick black smoke filled her lungs and stung her eyes. The heat from the flames seared the side of her face. Grabbing a bandanna from the back pocket of her denims, Mattie wet it down and tied it over the bridge of her nose.

She shouted to Slim. "I need to know where the horses are. I don't hear them. Check the pastures."

Coughing from the smoke, Mattie turned back to the well and found another bucket. Charley returned with several more buckets just as she finished filling the one she had found. Omaha appeared and they set up a brigade line with Mattie stationed beside the well.

During the moments when she wasn't filling buckets for Charley and Omaha, Mattie turned an angry gaze toward the blazing stable. She didn't believe that the fire was started by a careless ranch hand who left kerosene-soaked rags or a half-stepped-on cigarette by the bales of hay. The kerosene was kept in a small shed away from everything else. Her husband had been nothing if not careful when it came to combustibles such as oil and kerosene.

As for cigarettes, Charley was the only one of the three hired hands who smoked. Many times she'd seen Charley stub a half-finished cigarette out before he entered the barn. A few years ago, Mattie had teased Joe about how careful Charley was about smoking only outside. He'd answered solemnly that Charley's parents had died in a fire caused by his father smoking in bed.

So how did this fearsome fire get started? Could it have been started by Blackiston's lackeys? Maybe Capwell's henchmen had set the blaze. The only thing she was certain of was that it had to be sabotage.

The thrum of hoofbeats alerted Mattie. She stared off into the distance, but could not make out anyone yet. From the corner of her eye, she saw Omaha stiffen as he was returning with his empty bucket. Omaha handed the bucket to Slim, who had just returned to report that all the horses were safely in the far pasture. Omaha pulled a rifle from his saddle holster.

Mattie grabbed a pitchfork propped up against the well. Slim stood like a statue with the bucket in his hand until Omaha roughly urged him to continue throwing water on the flames while he and Mattie kept watch.

She glanced quickly over at what was left of the barn. It was a charred heap at this point. Mattie ducked her head so her ranch hands wouldn't see her tears of frustration that were welling up in her eyes. After she had control again, she walked over to Slim and laid the free hand on his arm, staying him from battling the flames.

"No point, Slim," she said shortly. "It's gone. We'll have to start rebuilding before winter."

Mattie swivelled her gaze toward the smoky darkness. A horse and rider emerged out of the haze. Light from the dying fire flickered over his lean and sober features. Omaha stood, tense, the rifle gripped in both hands as if ready to go into action at a moment's notice.

Omaha growled, "What's your business here, stranger?"

"I saw the fire from town and came here as fast as I could." The stranger eyed the smoking rubble that had once been the barn and remarked, "I guess I'm too late."

Omaha readied the rifle. "What do you really want around here, mister? I don't see anyone else from Rattlesnake beating down our doors to help us."

"My name is Jefferson Birch. I work for Tisdale Investigations." The stranger looked at Mattie and said, "You must be Mattie Quinn. You hired me."

She held her hand out toward the hostile ranch hand as if to keep him in check. "It's all right, Omaha. He's here to help."

Slim piped up. "How do we know he's who he says he is?"

"Fair enough," Birch conceded. "You folks are having trouble right now and you need proof." He reached inside his saddle pouch and produced a folded sheet of paper, extending it carefully to Mattie. He'd have shown them his Tisdale badge as well, if he'd remembered where it was.

She opened it and nodded. "He's who he says he is, all right. This is the letter I wrote to the agency requesting help."

Omaha didn't look convinced, but he nodded, his eyes squinted against the harsh smoky air. He said to Mattie, "You hired a gun?"

Birch answered. "I'd rather you didn't think of me as a hired gun. I investigate. I served for several years in the Texas Rangers."

Omaha was not impressed. "I'm sure plenty of Rangers left to hire out as killers."

Mattie interrupted. "Omaha, I really don't think . . ."

Charley piped up. "How do we know he isn't a spy sent here by Blackiston or Capwell?"

Omaha agreed and asked, "Why'd you leave the Rangers? That's a good job, I hear."

Birch's face hardened as he said, "I left for reasons that are nobody's business but mine."

Mattie couldn't understand why Omaha was acting so belligerent tonight. The other two were standing nearby, watching Omaha and this intruder exchange words. She watched all the men's eyes narrow as they sized each other up.

Charley and Slim looked away from Birch and shifted uncomfortably. Omaha lowered his rifle, avoiding Birch's steady gaze. Mattie took a deep breath and broke the uneasy silence with orders, giving everyone something to do.

"Charley, Slim, why don't you take Mr. Birch's horse out to the pasture with the others. Bring his saddle and pack up to the bunkhouse. Omaha," she said kindly, "I'd appreciate it if you'd give Mr. Birch your version of what's been happening here of late and don't leave out descriptions of Luther Capwell and Amos Blackiston."

Omaha nodded, pointed toward the bunkhouse, and said, "This way."

Before Birch could follow, Mattie touched his arm and said, "I sometimes wonder why I don't just sell this place to one of those . . . men, and get out. But I've just lost my husband—and I'm not about to let the ranch we built together be taken away from me as well." She stared out at the darkness and shook her head. Tears welled up in her eyes and Mattie averted her face so Birch wouldn't have to witness this display of sadness, anger, and frustration.

His voice was quiet and determined. "I can understand that, Mrs. Quinn. Right now, there's too many memories here for you to leave behind."

"You sound like you've left some memories behind, too, in Texas."

Birch answered with stone-faced silence, and Mattie realized she had spoken out of turn.

"My apologies, Mr. Birch. As you said, your reasons for leaving Texas are no one's business but your own."

There was a pause. "I do know how it feels to lose a loved one, Mrs. Quinn."

Mattie quickly wiped her tears away with a sleeve, then turned around to reply. She caught sight of his tall lean figure heading for the bunkhouse and a sense of security settled inside her. Mattie hadn't felt that way since . . . Suddenly she was ashamed of her attraction to this stranger. After all, she was newly widowed and Birch was only here to do a job.

But for the first time since Joe's death, Mattie felt that she had a chance of standing up to the enemy.

CHAPTER 4

AFTER Birch had taken leave of the widow, Omaha grudgingly filled him in on what had happened lately. They walked out toward one of the corrals downwind of the smoldering ruins of the barn. The night was crisp and clear, and Birch could see the stars bright in the dark fabric of the sky like a black and white gingham.

"Old Gumption wasn't good for anything except siring these days, but he meant a lot to Mattie." The lean blond man quickly corrected himself, "I mean, Mrs. Quinn. That bull was raised from a calf by Joe."

Birch ignored the hand's slip into the familiar. It was obvious that Omaha felt protective toward Mattie Quinn. That was good. At least we have one ally, Birch thought, if I can convince him that I'm here to help as well.

Birch said, "So the bull meant more than just another head for counting."

"He was the first longhorn they purchased and he's sired some pretty darn good beef over the last four years. He really wasn't all that old, either," Omaha explained. "But he was the oldest in the herd. We could always count on Old Gumption for stud work."

Birch couldn't understand how anyone could get so worked up over a bull, but he acknowledged that he'd never owned a cattle ranch either. "Did you bury him or something?"

Omaha looked at Birch like he was crazy and replied, "Of course not! We put most of him in the smokehouse and had some of Old Gumption for dinner tonight."

It was a fitting ending for Old Gumption, Birch thought,

who had given so much in his short life. Birch changed the subject. "Mrs. Quinn asked you to tell me about the two barons who made offers on her ranch."

Omaha nodded. "Luther Capwell and Amos Blackiston. They formed the Montana Cattlemen's Association about a year ago."

"Why was the Association formed?"

The ranch hand let out a laugh and said, "Well, if you asked Amos Blackiston or Luther Capwell, they'd tell you the Association was formed to protect cattlemen and also as a social organization."

"That sounds all right to me," Birch admitted.

Omaha was shaking his head. "Their real goal is to squeeze out the small ranchers. Most of the small ranchers like the Quinns worked hard for this land and they resent being told that they have no choice. Most of them would rather die."

"Has it come to that yet?"

The ranch hand shrugged and said, "Well, there've been two deaths, but they seem to be unrelated. Joe's, of course, has been called accidental. Mrs. Quinn says that she touched the rifle barrel just after she found him and it was cold."

Birch frowned. "And the marshal didn't check into it?"

Omaha let out a short bark of laughter. "No, most of Rattlesnake believes that Marshal Cobb is working for the Association."

"What do you think?"

Omaha shrugged. "I think that Gordy Cobb is a good man who's got himself in a bad situation. He's taking money from the Association to keep an eye on their cattle because there's been some rustling in these parts."

Birch nodded. If that were the case, then he understood Cobb well.

Omaha continued without prompting. "You wanted to know about Blackiston and Capwell. They're as different from each other as day and night." The hand leaned against a railing and looked up at the starry sky. "Amos Blackiston is a greedy bastard who's scared that someone's going to take advantage of him someday. That's why he wanted the Quinn property—for the water rights. He was afraid that Joe might use the creek as some kind of . . ." Omaha stopped as if he were searching for a word.

Birch filled it in. "Control?"

"Yeah, that's right, control."

Birch asked, "What about Luther Capwell?"

"Everyone likes him," Omaha shrugged. "No one has anything bad to say about Capwell."

The ranch hand was silent for a minute, so Birch prompted him. "But?"

Omaha looked up. "I don't like him. It's nothing I can put my finger on. I just get this unsettlin' feeling around him." He waved his hand in a dismissive gesture. "It's probably just me."

Maybe not, Birch thought.

Omaha showed Birch to an empty cot in the bunkhouse. It was like every other bunkhouse Birch had stayed in— cramped and dank with the sweat of a hard day's work clinging to the walls. And no matter how many lanterns were lit, the light seemed to be absorbed by the room instead of brightening it.

The thin mattress he slept on was filled with musty straw that needed to be shaken and aired outside for a few days, but he didn't complain. In fact, he dropped off to sleep almost immediately. He'd had no more than a few hours of sleep during his two-day ride. He'd spent most of his traveling time reading Mattie Quinn's letter to Tisdale Investigations and mulling over her story. The sense of urgency Birch had gotten from it made him all the more determined to get here before disaster struck again.

The next morning, Birch was up when the bell sounded for the morning meal. The hired hands were still grumbling about having to wake up as Birch left the bunkhouse and headed for the main house. The bleak weather was heavy with the promise of rain. He made a mental note to get his winter coat out of his bedroll before doing any riding today.

The front door was unlocked and he went on inside, following the sharp smell of bacon right to the table. Mattie Quinn came into the dining room from the kitchen with two full plates and set one down in front of him. The other one was apparently for herself. Birch looked hungrily at the eggs, grits, flapjacks, and bacon. He had to restrain himself from wolfing it down. Birch looked up and studied Mattie Quinn as she sat down at the table across from him.

She looked better in the morning light. Last night, all Birch had seen in the glow of the embers was her tangled hair and smudges of ash on her face. This morning she wore her freshly brushed hair caught up in a bandanna, presumably to keep it from getting into the food she cooked. It fell in dark waves around her shoulders. Mattie Quinn's hazel eyes were surrounded by long dark lashes. Faint freckles dotted her nose from working in the sun. All in all, she was a very beautiful woman, the kind of woman a man wanted to marry.

"I saw you coming over from the bunkhouse," she greeted him, seeming calmer than last night. "We usually serve ourselves at breakfast, but I wanted to talk to you before the others show up. I hope you slept well."

"I slept fine," he said. "Won't the others be coming in soon? We could wait and talk alone after we finish."

She waved a dismissive hand. "They had a long night last night, what with the fire and all. I'm actually surprised you got up so early."

"I don't need much sleep. Besides, I got a lot to do today. I wish I'd gotten here a little faster last night."

"You'd have been here in time to join the fire line," she sighed. "Frankly, Mr. Birch, I'm not sure why I hired you. What can you do for me? With all that's happened so far, whoever's terrorizing me has to be dangerous. I shouldn't have asked you to come."

"Tell me, if I were to get on my horse and ride out of here, what would you do?"

She set down her fork, closed her eyes briefly, and said reluctantly, "If they keep on tearing down my fences and butchering my cattle, I suppose I'd have no choice but to give in and sell the place."

"Where would you go to live?" Birch asked. "Do you have family?"

She shook her head. "No. But I could go back east or maybe buy another plot of land, I suppose, and start over."

Birch was silent for a moment, then said, "If you weren't being driven off, would you stay here?"

Birch watched her hands unconsciously clench and unclench. Then she got up from the table, walked over to the rough brick fireplace mantel, and touched it lovingly.

"Joe and I built this place with our bare hands," she said. "This is my home."

"Then I'll stay and help you," he said, adding, "but you'll have to help me as well."

She brightened visibly. "Anything. What can I do?"

Birch thought a moment, then said, "Omaha thinks Blackiston is behind it. I read your letter on the way up here and you mention two names: Amos Blackiston and Luther Capwell."

"Amos and Luther are the two biggest ranchers around here. They *own* Rattlesnake." She leaned forward and said quietly, "Mr. Birch, please remember that everything my hands say to you is in confidence. If it somehow gets around that he talked about Blackiston and Capwell in an unsavory manner, and if I'm forced out, Omaha would find it hard to get work around here. The same goes for Charley and Slim."

Somehow, Birch didn't think Omaha would mind if he were blackballed from the Blackiston and Capwell ranches. The former Texas Ranger got the impression that Omaha was smitten with the widow Quinn. If I stay around here much longer, Birch thought, I might feel that way myself.

So he nodded and asked, "Why do you suspect Blackiston and Capwell?"

Mattie Quinn lowered her eyes. "They want to buy my land. They made an offer to Joe and he turned them down. Then he died." She emphasized the last three words, paused, then continued. "The day after Joe's funeral, Amos came to see me to pay his respects and," she added bitterly, "to make an offer on my property."

She got up from the table and paced back and forth with her arms crossed. "Luther came later with another offer. I told both of them that I had no intention of selling."

Birch asked, "Did they make any threats?"

Mattie Quinn laughed and said, "Luther kept his counsel. He's not the kind of man who makes threats. There have been rumors that if he wants something, he'll just take it." She gave Birch a wry smile and added, "Of course, nothing's ever been proven. Now Amos, well, he's a different story altogether. When I turned his offer down, he flashed a nasty grin and said, 'Well, little lady, you may find running a ranch to be harder than you thought.' I ordered him to leave immediately because I couldn't be responsible for my actions."

Birch suppressed a smile. He could well imagine Mattie Quinn with a shotgun in her hands. Despite her earlier words of discouragement, she didn't seem to be easily intimidated.

He said, "It doesn't sound like much of a threat on Blackiston's part. Other than what you've told me, do you have any reason to suspect one more than the other?"

The Quinn widow turned to face Birch, her chin stubbornly set and her eyes flashing angrily. "Joe once told me that Amos was just greedy. He didn't like anyone to have power over him in any way."

Birch immediately understood and said, "And the fact that Rattler Creek runs right through your property before reaching his land means that you have control over him."

"I could dam up the creek if I had a mind to." She picked

up her fork and added pointedly, "And lately, I've thought long and hard about it."

"One last question: Does the marshal know what's going on out here?"

She smiled wryly and kept her eyes on her plate as she said, "I was wondering when we'd get around to Marshal Gordy Cobb. I don't have proof of it, but I'm positive my husband was killed by someone working for Blackiston or Capwell. Maybe both. When I tried to tell Cobb what I'd heard right before and after Joe was shot dead," she shook her head slowly, "he told me I was just an imaginative, grieving widow."

Birch recalled the widow Quinn's letter and asked, "That would be the horse you heard, right?"

She nodded and slowly looked up and met his eyes. "Right. Besides, half of the marshal's pay comes from Blackiston and Capwell. The laws don't apply to cattle barons who can afford to support the town marshal."

The kitchen door opened and two of the hired hands, Omaha and Slim, filed into the dining room with steaming plates of food. After a few respectful greetings to the widow Quinn and Birch, everyone fell silent and ate. Charley, looking surly, was the last to enter with his breakfast. Birch excused himself.

Mattie Quinn asked, somewhat anxiously, "What are you going to do first?"

He paused by the door and replied, "I'm going to check the remains of the barn and find out if the fire was an accident or deliberately set."

Omaha gave Birch a curious look and said, "But there's nothing left. Everything's been destroyed."

"If I were hired to set a barn on fire, I'd start with a tin of kerosene. Metal doesn't burn well." As Birch turned to leave, he noticed that everyone had stopped eating and were looking at one another with suspicion.

CHAPTER 5

IN the early morning light where a barn had once stood, a pile of charred debris lay with smoke still rising from it. A light rain promised to dampen the blackened rubble still further, so Birch could root around in it without much chance of burning his fingers when moving metal and wood out of his way.

The drizzle brought a chill to the autumn air. Down by the Rio Grande, the weather had mostly been fair to extremely hot, even in the fall and winter. On his travels he'd stuck to the southern territories from October to April. This was the farthest north he'd ever been. He was glad he'd bought a heavy, blanket-lined canvas coat when he'd been working in Wyoming. He'd brushed paint on it in an effort to windproof it, then packed it up with his bedroll for his journey up to Montana. Now was as good a time as any to break it in.

Birch entered the charred, wet ruins carefully, not wanting to disturb anything that might be a clue as to how the fire was started. He already suspected that it had been deliberately set by an unknown party.

Last night, Omaha had also told him that they didn't keep kerosene or oil in the barn. The only smoker on the ranch was Charley, who had watched his folks's home burn down— with his parents in it—because his father fell asleep in bed with a lit cigarette. Charley was very conscientious about stubbing cigarettes out before entering a building.

Birch continued to sift through the blackened bits of wood, charred saddles, and lumps of metal that might once have been horse bits or tools until he came to what might once have been a metal kerosene canister. The spout was melted as if the heat had been concentrated. Nothing remained of the rag that had probably been stuffed in the spout once the arsonist poured some of the contents on the bales of hay and lit them.

"You afraid of getting that pretty coat dirty, Birch?" Slim stood at the edge of the barnsite, leaning against a portion of barn that was miraculously still standing. He was shorter than Birch by six inches and had a slight paunch from either drinking or spending most of his time sitting in a saddle. He didn't fit his nickname, but then, cowpunchers had a very wry sense of humor. Slim looked like he was in his late twenties, although deep lines from outdoor living creased his baby face.

Birch stood up and held out the charred lump that had once been the kerosene container and asked, "Are you sure someone didn't leave a kerosene can in the barn yesterday?"

Slim entered the rubble. His face held no shadow of guilt, no furtive, hunted look. He examined the can closely, shaking his head.

"I don't understand it. Charley and me were together all day and we didn't bring anything into the barn besides hay." He frowned as he tried to recall yesterday. "We spent most of the day down at the river with some critters, checking their brands. Omaha was with us for most of the day, but he had to go back up to the house early to check on Mrs. Quinn. She was figuring the accounts up in the house by herself and we were all uncomfortable about leaving her alone . . ."

Birch finished Slim's thought: ". . . with everything that's happened lately."

"Even a small ranch like this needs more than three hands to run properly," Slim continued without prompting. "It's not so bad in the winter, but the spring and summer are when we make cattle runs south. Most of the time we sell the herd to the railroad companies near Helena, but some years we go as far south as St. Louis."

Birch nodded. He'd worked for enough ranches over the

past few years to get a general idea of how a cattle outfit was run. He usually found that hired hands were in high demand over the spring and summer months, and that only a select few were kept on during the cold months.

"Tell me about what's been happening on the ranch," Birch suggested.

Slim pulled up a piece of long grass and chewed on one of the ends. He said, "I thought Omaha gave you the lowdown last night."

"He did," Birch admitted, "but you were on your way back from Rattlesnake on the day Gumption was left on the doorstep as a warning. You might remember something that you didn't think was important at the time."

"Fine," Slim said. He headed for the corral. "But you're gonna have to ride along. I have work to do."

Birch followed. "You gonna do some outriding today?"

Slim's laugh was grim. "After what's been happening lately, what do you think? Someone's got to keep an eye on the widow's land."

He climbed over the split-rail fence easily and grabbed a set of reins that were hanging from a fencepost. Earlier this morning on his way to the main house for breakfast, Birch had noticed the cow ponies roaming around the pasture, sticking their heads between the fence rails and watching with curiosity anything that moved. Now there were only a few tired-looking rough-coated cayuses left. Most of the fresh horses had been smart enough to leave for the far end of the corral so they wouldn't be called on for a hard day's work "outriding."

Slim surveyed the lot and picked a horse feeding on a sparse clump of grass, seemingly oblivious to the cowboy's approach. Birch watched in amusement as Slim grasped the bit in his hand and held it out to a weary spotted cayuse.

"Come here, Jasper," Slim crooned. "Wouldn't you like a little iron candy?" The cowboy waggled the metal bit and sidled up to Jasper, who seemed indifferent to Slim. The horse eyed a clump of grass and began to work on it while the ranch hand got within five feet. Suddenly Jasper looked up, straight at Slim, whinnied softly, and moved off in search of more grass.

Slim's shoulders slumped, probably at the thought of spending more time courting the coy old cow pony. "Aw, stop fussing, you sway-backed, cross-eyed old bag of bones critter. You're no better than one of them longhorns you help look after. I ain't gonna . . . Stand still, damn you! I said stand still and I mean it."

Birch signaled to Slim and showed him how to corral Jasper with a minimum of trouble. A few minutes later, they were both saddled up.

"Where'd you learn to do that?" Slim asked Birch.

"When I was a Ranger, I had business in a small Mexican town. A Mexican soldier showed me the trick. When you think about it, it's just common sense. Ever since then, I've carried a carrot or apple for my horse. Works every time."

Slim shook his head in admiration.

They were approaching a herd of peacefully grazing longhorns. The leader, a mean-looking steer, looked up at the two men on horseback, then moved restlessly through his group as if informing them of the intrusion.

"That one's a troublemaker. He's drifted the herd a few times this summer. I'll be glad when we sell him at market in a few weeks."

Birch had some experience with "drifts" during his ranch work over the years. In the summer months, a drift usually started up after an aborted stampede or as a result of drought—scant food and water. He'd seen the aimless march of cattle go on for days as ranch hands stayed nearby, waiting for the herd to march itself into a barrier like a box canyon so it would turn around and march back until they became exhausted.

He'd never stayed on as a hired hand for the winter months, but he'd heard about them. The cattle would start the slow trance-like march through the snowdrifts, not stopping even if they broke through thin ice. They stared straight ahead, hypnotized, glassy-eyed, seemingly unaware that the cattle ahead of them had dropped into the freezing water or into a deep snowdrift. Sometimes it would be hundreds of cattle that died, sometimes only a few head.

The scruffy longhorn steer emitted a low warning sound meant for the two human intruders.

Birch decided it was time to get around to his purpose. "How do you see what's been happening around here? Do you think it's just coincidence, or could someone be trying to push Mrs. Quinn out of her home?"

Slim was silent for a minute, shaking his head thoughtfully. "At first I thought Joe's death was an accident. But then we started having all these other problems. I know Mrs. Quinn is new at ranching, but even a beginner don't have this many problems."

"Even a woman beginner?"

Slim let his breath out slowly. "Even for a woman. I mean, I admit I wasn't too crazy about having a woman boss on the ranch. Most rancher widows who stay on will let the ranch hands have run of the place. They keep to their place in the kitchen, making a home and raising children. But Mrs. Quinn's different. I reckon she needs to keep doing things. She can't sit in a chair making lace all day."

"So you're getting used to her involvement in the day-to-day running of the ranch."

"Yeah, me and Omaha. Now Charley is another matter entirely. Seeing as he's been ranch foreman for almost five years, I think he fully expected to take over when Mr. Quinn died."

Birch decided to probe deeper. "Is it possible that Joe's death was an accident like they say?"

Slim screwed up his face like he was thinking real hard. He said, "Now, I've worked here for near as long as Charley and I've never seen Mr. Quinn be careless with his Winchester."

Slim shook his head slowly and continued, "Mrs. Quinn swears that the barrel was cold when she touched it accidentally. I don't think the marshal thought to check the rifle—I know it didn't occur to any of us when we came up from the bunkhouse and saw Mr. Quinn. Probably wouldn't've done the marshal any good anyway because it was almost thirty minutes before he got there from Rattlesnake."

"Why wasn't the cold barrel brought up to the marshal?"

"Mrs. Quinn did try to bring up a few of those points the next day, but Marshal Cobb, he don't want to know about it. He'd already made up his mind."

Birch couldn't understand it, so he asked, "Why didn't one or more of you step forward with some of this information?"

Slim sounded weary. "It wouldn't have done us no good, Birch. Mrs. Quinn knows that. Fact is, Omaha offered to come forward and I said if he did, I would. But she didn't want us to be in any danger on her account. So we respected her wishes." He brightened momentarily, showing a gap-toothed grin. "Fine-lookin' woman, ain't she? Once her mournin' is over with, I have half a mind to go courtin'."

Birch ignored Slim's ruminations about the widow Quinn and concentrated on the information he'd gathered. If Mattie Quinn had allowed Omaha and Slim to come forward with the information and it had backfired, as it most assuredly would have with a lawman in the pay of two cattle barons, Slim and Omaha's lives would have been in danger for speaking up. They would probably have had to leave the county and Mattie would be out two ranch hands. She would have a hard time defending herself against whichever ruthless cattle king was trying to drive her off of her land.

And that brought Birch's thoughts to Charley. Where did he fit in? Slim had said Charley wasn't happy with Mattie Quinn's unorthodox need to learn about running the ranch, yet he stayed on. Could he have had anything to do with trying to run her out? But that would mean he'd be out of a job. Of course, a good foreman could always find work elsewhere. Birch wasn't sure about him yet.

He brought himself back to the present and asked Slim, "What do you think of Amos Blackiston?"

The ranch hand took his hat off and scratched his scalp uncomfortably. The sun had burnt off the morning chill and the rest of the day promised to be cloudless and warm. Birch wished he'd left his coat behind. He pulled it off and secured it behind him on his saddle.

"Gee, Birch, do I have to say anything? I think I've said too much already."

"This won't go any farther than you, me, and the horses," Birch reassured him. "I just need to know what kind of men I'm dealing with. Mattie Quinn gave me some idea, but she has more reason to dislike them than you do. Are either Blackiston or Capwell the kind of men who'd kill a small rancher to get his land?"

Slim didn't hesitate to say, "Blackiston would in a minute. I don't know about Capwell. He seems like a decent fellow. Look, Birch. You heard what I said about the marshal being in Blackiston and Capwell's pay. It's not that Marshal Cobb is a bad man. He's very good about keeping the town of Rattlesnake law abiding. But when it comes to justice, well, he just can't be trusted to be fair."

Birch nodded and replied, "But you still haven't told me about either Blackiston or Capwell. What do you know about them?"

"Amos Blackiston will do anything to get what he wants. Capwell, well, I won't make the man out to be a saint. There's been some rumors, but nothing that's been proven. They say that Blackiston has a man on his payroll who does all his dirty work and he does it quietlike so you never know what hit you. Calls his hired gun a detective for the Cattlemen's Association."

Birch asked, "What's this detective supposed to be doing for the Association?"

"Oh, track down stolen cattle and cow horses, turn in rustlers, that sort of thing."

Birch reached a conclusion. "So it looks like Amos Blackiston has the most reason to want to drive Mattie off her land."

"Oh, I didn't say that," Slim replied.

Birch argued, "But you said Blackiston has a hired gun and would do anything to get what he wanted."

"But that's true of Luther Capwell as well. And he's been known to use Blackiston's hired gun when he needs something done. But, Blackiston's land runs south of Mrs. Quinn's and he's been worried that she'll dam the water up on him sometime."

Birch decided he'd better pay a visit to Amos Blackiston.

CHAPTER 6

AFTER talking to Mattie and the ranch hands, Birch was fairly certain that even if Amos Blackiston wasn't behind Joe Quinn's death, he was behind the barn burning and the mutilated steer. He had the strongest motive and by all accounts was ruthless and greedy.

As he rode toward the Blackiston ranch, Birch ran through all the events again. It was almost too easy, he thought. He was reminded of how routine most of the cases he'd worked on in Texas had been—he'd spent most of his time tracking robbers and rustlers. The few murder cases that Birch had been brought in on had been straightforward—a man kills his wife in a rage, or neighbors argue over territory and one of them uses his shotgun to make his point.

As he headed in the general direction of the Blackiston property, Birch caught a quick movement across Rattler Creek. It was hard to tell whether or not it was a man, but Birch decided to play it safe. He reined Cactus in near a copse of trees and hovered near an aspen, just out of firing range. Another rustle of movement attracted his attention and before he could reach for his gun, a pronghorn antelope bounded into sight and went on its way. Birch watched the proud animal run swiftly toward a grassy range beyond the thicket of trees from which it had emerged. His gun hand relaxed, Birch remounted Cactus and continued on, intent on his destination.

As Birch expected, the Blackiston ranch was much larger than Mattie Quinn's. If the great expanse of prairie he passed on his way to the main house was any indication, Blackiston was a wealthy man. There must have been two hundred cattle milling around the range, probably only a tenth of the stock Blackiston had, Birch figured.

The main house confirmed his estimation of Amos Blackiston's wealth. Out of context with its harsh surroundings, the house was fitted with imported glass windows, a coat of white paint, and, out in front, the beginnings of a flower garden. To Birch, this indicated that Blackiston was married to a woman who longed to bring a little civilization to this rough country.

A buggy with black fringe stood in the clearing, making it clear that someone was either preparing to leave or had just come back from somewhere. Birch guessed that the buggy was also the wife's idea. A man only rode in one of those things if he was courting or was citified.

"What do you want, stranger?" A large man with a nose that had been in one too many fights appeared from around the side of the house, a shotgun hanging easily from his side. "We're not hiring this late in the season. In fact, we'll be sending most of our hands away in a few weeks."

He gave no indication by his tone that he was looking for trouble, but seemed quite aware of Birch's guns and willing to shoot if this trespasser made any suspicious moves.

Birch got right to the point. "I'm not looking for work. I'm here to see Mr. Blackiston on other business."

"Mr. Blackiston's business is my business."

Before Birch could answer, a man on horseback appeared. The horse was a big sleek bay and the rider didn't look like he belonged on such a beautiful animal. He was a grossly overweight man with a little red nose. Birch saw a gleam of authority mixed with greed in those little piggy eyes that told him he'd just met Amos Blackiston.

The guard looked up at the fat man and nodded, then addressed the large man on the bay. "Mr. Blackiston, sir, this man was just about to leave. I'm seeing to that right now."

The horse seemed to sigh as Amos Blackiston dismounted

and said, "Thank you, Wiley. I'll be in the study if you need
me."

Birch called out, "Mr. Blackiston, I've come here on behalf
of Mattie Quinn."

Blackiston paused for a second before handing the reins
to Wiley. His smile was neutral as he replied, "Oh, I see. I
guess she's finally come to her senses. Well, come on in." The
big man gestured for Birch to follow him inside the house.

"Mr. Blackiston," Wiley called out, glaring menacingly at
Birch, "do you want me to tag along?"

The cattle baron waved his bodyguard toward the barn,
saying, "No, I don't think I'll be needing you. You take care
of my bay. Make sure Pete's fed well."

They entered the house and Birch was shown into the
library. The pleasant smells of leather and cedar lingered.
Blackiston strode over to the windows and threw open the
heavy, imported brocade curtains. Dust fluttered lazily in the
strong rays of sunlight that streamed through the glass
panes.

Blackiston sneezed and wiped his nose with a handy bandanna. "I wish that wife of mine wouldn't close those curtains
during the day. I sneeze every time I have to open them." He
faced Birch again. "Now, what did you come here for? And
what did you say your name was?"

Birch said calmly, "I didn't say. But my name is Jefferson
Birch. And I'm here on Mattie Quinn's behalf. She's been
having some trouble lately with her ranch."

Amos Blackiston let out a bleating laugh. "Well, of course
she is. She's a woman. Women aren't meant to do range
work." He leaned forward, his arms supported by his desk
surface. "What kind of money is she asking?"

Birch eyed Blackiston's ample figure and decided he was
even less capable of doing range work than Mattie Quinn.
"None."

Blackiston blinked and replied, "She's not ready to sell?

Why the hell are you here then? Maybe I should have had my ranch hand throw you off my property after all."

"Mrs. Quinn is doing fine running her ranch," Birch said. "But last night someone burned her barn down."

"Oh, now ain't that a shame," Blackiston said with a slight smile and shake of the head. "That little woman's had such trouble over the past few months, what with her husband getting himself killed and making her a widow. It ain't right, a pretty young thing like that being stuck on a ranch, doing man's work and all." He poured himself a brandy. Birch noticed that he wasn't offered one. Blackiston continued, "Last July, I had a range fire. Ten acres of good grassland burned up during the hottest month of the year. It's something we all have to live with."

"This fire was deliberately set. The horses had all been removed from their stables and led to the far north pasture to graze."

The ranch owner shrugged. "Someone just forgot to bring the horses in for the night."

Birch replied, "Omaha swears he brought them all in. This morning I found what was left of a kerosene can where the barn once stood."

Again Amos Blackiston shrugged. "Anyone could have left kerosene in the barn. They have to fill their lanterns. I can assure you that my workers forget the occasional kerosene can in my barn, too."

Birch said evenly, "No one at that ranch left it in the barn. They all know how touchy that stuff is, even if the weather has cooled off."

"Hired hands have been known to lie when it suits their purposes," Blackiston said, took another swig of his brandy, and came out from behind his desk to stand toe to toe with Birch. It was an unnerving move and Birch had a sudden understanding of one of the reasons Blackiston had done so well for himself. When it came to the business of buying and selling livestock, he probably used the same trick to intimidate.

But such bluster did not work on Birch. He looked the cattle baron steadily in the eye and asked, "And what about the mutilation of the Quinn prize bull? The way I have it figured, the man who did that was the same one who killed Joe Quinn a few months ago."

Blackiston's voice got very quiet. "Are you accusing me of something? Because if you are, I'll have the law on you so fast you'll be fifty miles from Sunday before you realize you were run out of town for slanderous damn talk like that."

Birch kept steady eye contact with the cattle king. "I don't like threats, Mr. Blackiston."

The fat man pulled back a bit and drained his brandy, immediately refilling it. "What reason would I have to kill Joe Quinn, let alone to terrorize his widow?"

"You made an offer on their property."

Blackiston laughed as he poured a brandy and handed it to Birch. "That's not a crime. That was good business."

Birch accepted the brandy reluctantly, but didn't drink it right away. "No, it's not a crime to make an offer on some land, but murder is a crime. A hanging crime." Birch sipped his brandy. "And I've been told by some folks around here that you're a man who doesn't take no for an answer. You get what you want, no matter what."

Blackiston's jaw tightened, showing that Birch was beginning to annoy him again. Suddenly he relaxed and clapped a hand on Birch's shoulder. "I like you, Birch. You're a man who doesn't back down. How would you like a job on my ranch? I'm sure I can find room for you."

"I already have a job."

"I'll double whatever Mattie Quinn pays you," he said heartily.

Birch repeated, "I already have a job with Mrs. Quinn. And I think you've answered my questions about who's behind all the problems on the Quinn ranch. And who killed Joe Quinn."

Blackiston's face got hard again. "I don't go around killing people and setting stables on fire."

Birch smiled coldly. "No, you hire people to do it."

The ranch owner narrowed his eyes. "If you're just a hired hand with the widow Quinn, why ask all of these questions? Why turn down a better offer from a bigger ranch? Are you more than you appear to be," Blackiston flashed Birch a terrible smile, "Jefferson Birch?"

Birch realized he'd overplayed his hand. He said, "I just like to avoid trouble and I'm here on behalf of Mattie Quinn. She respectfully requests you leave her the hell alone."

"Why doesn't she go to the marshal with her problems?" Blackiston asked. "Why come to me? I'm not the law."

"But you own the law," Birch replied.

The big cattle baron let out a cruel laugh and said, "You can't prove that. We have nothing further to discuss." Blackiston was about to turn his back on Birch when he added, "I just decided I don't want you working for me, Birch. Get the hell off my ranch."

Birch drained his brandy in one swallow, set the glass down on a nearby table, and jammed his hat back on his head. There was nothing more to be said so he walked out.

As Birch opened the front door, he almost ran into a young woman who was coming inside. She had laughing eyes, a Roman nose, and a plump, pretty figure. Her auburn hair was wind-tossed as if she'd just been riding. If this was Amos Blackiston's daughter, she must have taken after her mother.

He took his hat off and stepped aside to let her in. She smiled at him and was about to speak when Amos Blackiston came roaring out of his library.

"Birch! I'll . . ." He stopped when he saw the young woman and addressed her. "Mabel, what are you doing here?"

"Hi, Papa." She had a sweet voice that matched her smile. "I just came in from my afternoon ride."

"Oh. Well, why don't you run along and see if your mother needs your help."

Blackiston beamed with a paternal glow until Mabel was out of sight, then turned back to Birch with malice in his eyes and said, "I thought you'd left by now, Birch."

"And good day to you, too," Birch muttered. He headed for his horse, looking back once more. Blackiston caught the eye of several cowhands nearby and gave a discreet nod.

The guard, Wiley, was among them and he stepped up to Birch, his shotgun still in his hands. Birch studied the big man. Wiley was as large as Amos Blackiston, but his size came from muscle, not soft living.

"I'm leaving," Birch replied and turned toward his horse.

A steel hand grabbed his upper arm, spinning him around to face the grim ranch guard. "You look like a troublemaker to me," Wiley said, shoving Birch back against Cactus's saddle.

Birch could feel anger burning slowly in him, but he decided here was not the place to start a fight. If Wiley wanted to start something down at the saloon in Rattlesnake, Birch would be happy to oblige him. But here, on Blackiston's ranch, he'd seen too many ranch hands around, and figured that if they were half as loyal as Wiley appeared to be, the odds weren't in Birch's favor that he'd leave under his own steam.

So instead of taking a crack at the ranch hand's jaw, Birch roughly brushed Wiley's hand away. As he started to mount Cactus, something hard cracked across his skull and he staggered into the nearby split-rail fence.

Birch's vision blurred for a few moments, then cleared in time to see the beefy guard coming at him with a murderous look on his face. Grabbing the fence for support, Birch hoisted himself up and caught Wiley in the gut with his boot. The hired man grunted in surprise as he sprawled out on the ground and dropped his shotgun. Birch moved toward his attacker, kicking the gun away to keep the fight fair. Out of the corner of his eye, he saw a small group of Blackiston's men gathering for the fight.

Wiley growled when he saw Birch approaching and tried to stand. Birch reached him before Wiley was on his feet, and hit a left to Wiley's jaw. He looked around to see if anyone else was going to take him on as well, then glanced toward Blackiston's house. The movement of the library curtain caught his eye. So Amos Blackiston was watching. Or was it Mabel Blackiston flicking the curtains back in place before her father caught her observing the ungentlemanly acts in front of the house?

He turned his back for a third time and headed for Cactus. This time Birch was warned of Wiley's attack by an eager spectator.

"Get 'im, Wiley!" urged a skinny, buck-toothed boy.

Birch easily sidestepped Wiley's clumsy dive, but the guard managed to grab his ankles. Birch stumbled and fell hard on his right hip. Now he wished he'd taken his gunbelt off earlier. Wiley landed on top of him and started pounding at Birch's face with powerful fists. The ex-Ranger flipped his opponent off balance and drove his fist into Wiley's gut, then a left to his chin, leaving Wiley too winded and too hurt to fight any longer.

As Birch dusted himself off, he looked around at the sea of disappointed faces. He sized them up one by one, but soon realized that Wiley had been the biggest of the lot. Realizing that no one else was going to challenge his ride out of here, Birch headed for Cactus.

A wide-eyed Mabel Blackiston emerged from the front door just as he mounted up. With a tip of his hat to her, Birch headed back to the Quinn ranch.

What he had accomplished with Blackiston was almost nothing. No, that wasn't quite right. Blackiston now thought

that Mattie Quinn had a hired gun on her ranch. But it
didn't appear to frighten him a single bit. In fact, he guessed,
it seemed to have just made him more determined to get
Mattie Quinn's land any way he could.

her was a lawyer and I drafted it along similar lines to a
:ument I found among his effects. We just need a
ness . . ."

Amos's cold smile stopped her flow of words. "I'm sure it's
order. I just won't sign it. I want your land as well as the
ter rights. I want to build an empire and I won't let
ybody, particularly a woman, stand in my way. Now if
u're interested in selling it, this is my offer." He wrote
wn an amount and handed it to her.

The widow Quinn glanced at it briefly, then looked up at
m with contempt. "But this is less than the last offer."

"And the offers will continue to dwindle until you sell."
mos drained his third bourbon and felt the warmth spread
roughout his body. "You see, I can't lose. And your Mr.
irch won't stand in my way much longer, either."

He stood up and came around to the front of the desk to
and over the widow Quinn, a smile of supreme confidence
n his face as he dropped the document in her lap. "You'd
etter leave now. We have nothing further to say to each
ther. I'll keep this last offer open to you until tomorrow
oon. Then it goes down again."

Amos Blackiston was pleased to note that his intimidation
ad left Mattie Quinn's face drained of color. She managed
o stand up and leave with dignity.

Through the window, he watched her mount up and ride
ff his property. There was something satisfying in threat-
ning a woman, especially a widow as pretty and independent
s Mattie Quinn. Amos replayed the look on her face just
efore she turned and left. He wanted to see her crawling
back to him and taking a pittance for her land, a tenth of
what it was really worth.

Amos took his pocket watch out and noticed that he had
time for another drink before dinner. As he sipped this one,
Amos started planning what he'd do tomorrow. He'd have to
find out about this Jefferson Birch. Tomorrow would be a

CHAPTER 7

AMOS Blackiston was angry when that upstart, Jefferson
Birch, left. They had a few words during which Birch prac-
tically got Amos to admit that he was responsible for the
widow Quinn's troubles. After that, Amos stomped back into
his study.

He was still mad while he ate his midday meal and snapped
at his wife and daughter when they tried to tell him about
the fight that had gone on outside the house between Wiley
and that stranger who'd been here earlier. And he was still
mad when Mattie Quinn showed up a few hours later.

That Birch fellow had made him plenty angry, sticking his
nose into other people's affairs. Amos would have to set him
straight after getting the Quinn widow out of the way. That
was the first order of business, after all. The thought that he
was getting another chance to intimidate Joe Quinn's widow
didn't calm him down much.

She stood on his doorstep in ranch clothes that were
obviously her dead husband's work clothes because of the
loose fit. The denims had been cinched tightly around her
shapely waist with a belt. There was something very appeal-
ing about the way Mattie Quinn was dressed, and for a
moment, Amos wished his wife and daughter had gone to
town for the day. He'd like to show the widow Quinn what it
was like to be with a man again.

Instead, he asked, "What do you want, Mrs. Quinn?"

"I've come to talk to you about a few things."

A triumphant feeling swept over him as he ushered her
into his study. Had she met with Birch and, after seeing her

49

battered hired gun, realized that trying to save her ranch was useless?

Amos closed the doors for complete privacy.

"Please sit," he said, indicating a comfortable-looking leather wing chair with a well-worn cushion. He pulled a bottle of Kentucky bourbon and two glasses out of his bottom desk drawer and held the amber liquid up. "Bourbon?"

Mattie sat down and shook her head. "No, thank you."

He poured a liberal amount for himself and asked, "Why are you here?"

Her mouth compressed, becoming a straight line. "I've come to make you an offer. I believe that Jefferson Birch, my . . . hired hand, was here for a visit today."

Amos replied shortly, "I met him."

Mattie Quinn leaned back in her armchair. Her expression relaxed slightly. "Good. He knows his business." She looked directly at Amos and added, "I feel very secure around him."

Amos decided not to beat around the bush any longer. He raised his eyebrows and drawled, "Don't tell me you've hired yourself a gunslinger, Mrs. Quinn! I wouldn't have thought you'd do a thing like that."

She got out of the chair, paced the floor, and said, "Mr. Birch was hired by me in connection with the ranch."

Amos decided to go along with Mattie Quinn's little game for now. "Yes, that's what he told me." He watched carefully as a look of relief passed over her face, then added, "But I don't believe a word of it. Mr. Birch is more than he appears to be."

The widow Quinn smiled with confidence as she sank back down into the leather armchair. "What Jefferson Birch has done in the past is none of my affair."

"Then why did he come here and demand that I leave you alone?"

She shot back triumphantly, "He's loyal." They stared at each other for a minute before she continued, "You deny

involvement in the death of my husband and you a chance to prove it."

With a virtuous smile, Amos replied, "I hav will tell you that I was nowhere near your ra husband died. The marshal declared it an ac We have nothing to discuss."

A grim widow Quinn leaned over his desk nesses have been known to lie." She straight and said, "But I'm not here to accuse you of m

Amos drained his bourbon and poured an was getting annoyed with this conversation ar she would leave. "I don't have time for thi business."

"I've come here today with this." She withdre from her shirt pocket and tossed it on Amos's

He shrugged. "What is this?" He picked it up scanned it.

Mattie Quinn explained, "Before he died, Joe he thought you were interested in our ranch be Creek runs through our land before it goes t property and that you might be afraid that we'd up and keep all that water to ourselves."

Amos nodded tersely. "The thought had mind."

Mattie's laugh was hollow. "I've drawn up a regarding rights to the creek."

Amos took it from her and glanced at it with "Sum it up for me."

She said, "Basically, it states that we share the v and I can't divert the creek without your permissi versa. Now, we just need someone to witness it. Pe daughter or a ranch hand?"

Amos shook his head. "I won't sign it." He hand to her.

Mattie Quinn looked at him with astonishment a back the document. "But it would be perfectly lega

good time to ride into Rattlesnake and send out some wires to a couple of influential people who owed him a few favors.

Amos would find out soon enough just what Jefferson Birch was all about. Maybe he'd find something hidden in Birch's past that could be used against him. Then again, maybe he'd find out that Birch was clean and he'd just have to kill him. Amos would regret having to kill Birch because the man appeared to have his uses. But, he dismissed Jefferson Birch from his mind and concentrated on the present. He'd finished his work for the day and decided to ride around the immediate area, surveying his domain.

A bruised and battered, but mostly recovered, Wiley brought his boss's horse out and Amos rode off to the back forty acres toward Rattler Creek. On the other side of the creek, the faded meadowland rolled gently out to meet a steep-sided butte in the distance. Amos could see a herd of his longhorns on the flat land below the stream. Very faintly, he could hear his ranch hands answer each other over the bellowing cattle. If he squinted, Amos could even make out the camp with the cook stirring a pot of what was probably beans and bacon.

It was quiet near the creek except for the constant, busy sound of running water. Amos realized that he hadn't been fishing in quite a while. He had a sudden overwhelming yearning for fish. Maybe he'd take a pole down here tomorrow and catch a couple of trout or bass for breakfast.

It was almost time for supper, according to Amos's pocket watch, so he started back for the house. When he was almost home, he heard thundering hooves behind him.

Who could be running his horse like that? It had to be important. Amos guided his mount to the side of the makeshift trail and turned to witness whoever was riding so urgently. The horse and rider broke through a clump of trees about a hundred yards away from Amos.

He recognized the rider and chided him for being so

reckless. "What in tarnation are you doing here? I thought we agreed that you'd stay away from here for a time."

The rider smiled humorlessly and drew his gun. Amos reached for his and realized that he'd left the house without his protection. How could he be so stupid? He cursed himself for being a damn fool as the rider fired.

Amos felt the first bullet burn as it entered his gut, but he only heard, rather than felt, the next two shots. Through a haze, Amos wondered if anyone had heard and if they would investigate where the gunshots came from.

Clutching his big stomach in an attempt to keep the blood from leaking out, Amos grimaced as he tumbled off his horse. "Damn you! I thought you worked for me."

The killer grinned as he said to the dying man, "I got a better offer."

CHAPTER 8

MATTIE returned late in the afternoon to an empty main house. The sun was setting and the ranch hands would be back with hearty appetites. It was time to prepare the evening meal. Mattie's hands trembled when she started chopping the onions and potatoes for a stew, so she set the knife down and took a deep breath.

A sudden sound from outside took her by surprise. I must calm down, she thought. Slim, Charley, and Omaha were still out rounding up the cattle for the impending drive, so Mattie grabbed a shotgun from the kitchen door, the one she'd placed there after Joe was killed, and peered out toward the barnsite. All was quiet, then a moment later Jefferson Birch appeared in the ruins of the barn, emerging from behind half of a charred wall.

Mattie sighed with relief and returned the shotgun to the crude wall rack. She'd almost forgotten about the detective. Anxiety hit her. Birch had been to see Blackiston a few hours before she rode out there. Wanting to keep her visit to Amos Blackiston a secret, she had taken a little-used trail to the cattle baron's ranch, but Birch was no fool. Suppose he asked questions at dinner about where she'd been this afternoon— what would she tell him?

Mattie felt like a traitor hiding her visit from Birch, but there didn't seem to be any point in telling him now. Not after she'd failed so miserably in eliciting information from the cattle baron. She had hoped if Blackiston thought she'd hired a gunslinger to protect her ranch, the threat of Birch would make the cattle baron back off. And maybe she'd have gotten him to admit to something, anything that would

55

implicate him in Joe's death, but she hadn't known how to go about it.

Instead, she'd blathered on about water rights. He must have seen through her thinly veiled excuse for a visit because he'd been so cold, so vicious to her. It was obvious that he'd enjoyed intimidating the young widow.

Mattie pulled out the legal document and stared at it, realizing what a foolish idea it had been. Now she'd probably lose Birch's trust as well. Thinking back, she couldn't remember meeting anyone on the road or at the ranch. It was a long shot, but she didn't think that Blackiston would be talking to Birch anytime soon.

There was only a moment of hesitation before she stuffed it into the wood-burning stove and watched it reduced to ashes, her heart pounding a wild frightened beat as she realized that she had put Jefferson Birch in danger by letting Blackiston think the detective was better with a gun than he probably was. How would she handle that? She had to warn Birch that Blackiston would come gunning for him. But if she did, she'd have to tell Birch where she'd been and why.

Mattie started slicing apples for a pie, her dilemma whirling around in her head. While the pie was baking, she went over to the kitchen door and watched Birch poking around in the barn ruins. He would pause now and again to pass his hand over his hair. From her vantage point, she could only just make out that his jeans and cotton shirt were smudged with cold gray ash. Stubble darkened his lantern jaw.

When Birch was deep in thought, he reminded Mattie of Joe. She stared at the distant mountains, organizing her thoughts and fighting the desire she felt for Birch.

When she caught sight of the three ranch hands driving a herd into one of the far corrals, Mattie sounded the dinner bell. When Birch reached the table, everyone was discussing the cattle drive and whether Mattie should join it or stay here on the ranch.

"Mr. Birch. I'm so glad you could join us." Mattie greeted

him pleasantly as she handed him a plate laden with savory stew and biscuits. Glancing briefly at his face, she noticed his battle scars for the first time, and asked apprehensively, "What happened to your face?"

He grinned and said, "I ran into the right end of a shotgun."

The three ranch hands guffawed. Mattie cocked her head to one side and said, "Looks to me like it was the wrong end."

Birch shook his head with a straight face and replied, "No, ma'am. The wrong end would have put me in a pine box."

"Did you find out anything today?"

Mattie and the others listened as Birch told them about his visit, and the fight with Amos Blackiston's guard, Wiley, and the threat to attack Mattie's ranch.

Omaha looked at Birch in disgust, then addressed Mattie. "See, Mrs. Quinn? He's no help at all. All he does is stir up trouble. Any more of this and he might get us all killed. It's not too late to ask Birch to leave. I'll see that he's off your property before morning."

Mattie turned to Birch and raised her eyebrows in a silent plea. Before she could ask him if Omaha might not be right, Birch put his fork and knife down and said, "He's partly right, Mrs. Quinn. I am stirring things up and it is dangerous. But it's the only way to shake the killer enough so that he eventually makes a mistake. Most likely that'll mean he'll come after you. But you could just decide to sell your place. I could leave first thing in the morning."

Mattie was silent while she wrestled with this new predicament. She already knew Blackiston would come after her. If Birch's visit hadn't spurred the cattle king into action, her visit certainly would make sure of that. Of course, she could just sell the ranch for Blackiston's less-than-acceptable offer and be done with it. Her thoughts turned briefly to Joe. The loss of the barn and the bull were something she could have

lived with, but to have her husband taken away from her—
no, she had to stay and fight it out. She was in it this far.

Finally, she turned to her hired men and said, "I'm sorry,
but Mr. Birch stays. You are all free to leave anytime. But I
have to see this through. I have to trust Mr. Birch. I know
we're in a bad situation, but I've weighed the trouble he's
stirred up against what's already happened."

She recited, "Joe was killed. His prize bull was slaughtered.
The barn was set on fire." Mattie shrugged. "That all happened before Mr. Birch arrived. It can't get much worse."

There was some grumbling from all three hands, but in
the end, they all agreed to stay.

Toward the end of supper, they heard a horse approaching. Mattie rose from her half-finished slice of apple pie to
find out who was visiting at the supper hour. It was a grim-
looking Marshal Cobb.

She opened the door and called out harshly, "What are
you doing here, Marshal? Haven't you done enough
already?"

Something in his expression made her realize that Marshal
Cobb wasn't here on a social visit.

Gordy Cobb took his hat off in deference to her and said,
"I'm sorry to trouble you again, Mrs. Quinn, but it's important. May I come in?"

She sighed, feeling put out by the lawman's unwelcome
appearance. He followed her into the dining room where
Birch and the ranch hands sat at the table listening to
Charley tell a raucous joke. They all looked up at Cobb,
curiosity in their eyes. Mattie felt a twinge of foreboding as
the lawman nodded his head in greeting to all the men, his
gaze lingering on Jefferson Birch.

Then he announced, "Amos Blackiston was murdered
tonight."

Mattie blanched and grabbed the edge of the table, then
sank into her chair. The three ranch hands stopped all

activity, forks full of apple pie poised in mid-air. Birch's inscrutable gray eyes never left the lawman.

Cobb scrutinized Birch as he said, "I understand that you paid a visit to Amos this afternoon."

Birch nodded. "That's right."

Cobb looked down at his hat, the wide brim smooth from rubbing it between his fingers. "I have reason to believe that someone visited Amos Blackiston after you left. Plenty of people saw you leave the first time, but you could have doubled back and killed him."

"I had nothing more to say to Amos Blackiston," Birch replied. "What possible reason would I have for killing him?"

The marshal cocked his head in Mattie's direction and said, "I understand that you work for Mrs. Quinn here as a sort of, shall we say, hired gun."

"Wrong," Birch answered. "People assume what they want to assume. I've been hired to look into Joe Quinn's death. I'm a detective in the employ of Tisdale Investigations. This afternoon, I visited Amos Blackiston to let him know that Mrs. Quinn was not about to be intimidated into selling her ranch."

Cobb asked, "And his answer?"

Birch made a wry face and touched one of the bruises on his face. "Well, it was more of a threat. My impression was that he was behind most of it. He told me in so many words that if I didn't move on soon, I'd catch a good case of bullet fever."

Cobb straightened up, tugging at his gunbelt, and replied, "Well it looks as though Amos Blackiston was the one who caught a case of that. I'd be inclined to believe you, Birch, but you're a stranger here. Most of the townspeople, when they catch wind of what's been going on, are more likely to side with the Blackistons against you, despite the fact that you've been hired by Mattie Quinn."

Mattie interrupted, "Why not, Marshal?"

"Well," Marshal Cobb rubbed his neck thoughtfully, "now

don't get me wrong, Mrs. Quinn, because I didn't like Amos Blackiston, either. But I've known Amos longer than I've known Birch."

Mattie gave the lawman a stare filled with contempt. If Marshal Cobb didn't like Blackiston all that much, she thought, why was he taking money from the rancher? Didn't he know that made him untrustworthy in the eyes of the other ranchers?

Cobb continued, "The townsfolk are going to say that you were hired by a widow given to hysterical imaginings that her husband was murdered. By Amos Blackiston, no less. And no matter what you call yourself, you're still a hired gun to me. Your alibi is good until you clobbered Wiley and left the Blackiston ranch. But as I said before, you could have come back again and killed him."

Mattie resented Cobb's description of her. She wasn't about to let her only hope, Birch, go to jail—even if he did kill Blackiston. She asked, "Marshal, when was Amos killed?"

"The shot was heard about two hours ago. Guess he's been dead about that long."

Here was a golden opportunity to alibi herself as well as do Birch a good turn. She stuck her chin out stubbornly and said, "Well, Mr. Birch couldn't have done it. He was with me in the library. We were discussing Amos Blackiston. Mr. Birch thought a group of Blackiston men would come out here tonight and attack us."

Out of the corner of her eye, Mattie saw Charley start to protest, but Slim kicked him under the table. Charley held his tongue. Omaha narrowed his eyes at Birch and tensed as if he were going to leap across the table at the detective's throat.

Cobb stuck his hat back on and nodded to the widow Quinn. "Well, ma'am," he said, "you could have called on me. I wouldn't have let that happen."

Mattie Quinn replied frostily, "Why, Marshal, I thought

you didn't believe me. I'm just a hysterical, imaginative widow, remember?"

Cobb looked sheepish. He said, "Well, ma'am, I guess I'll have to take your word that Birch was with you. For now."

He turned to face Birch and said, "You're free for right now, but I may be back to ask you more questions. Don't leave the area."

Birch nodded and said, "I'm not going anywhere."

After the lawman left, Birch turned to Mattie. "You shouldn't have lied on my account. I would have gone with him to Rattlesnake and he would have wired Arthur Tisdale for information."

She widened her eyes and tried to look earnest. "But we need you here. Especially with Blackiston dead. Could the same person who killed him . . . ?"

She didn't have to finish her thought. No one finished their pie, either. News of another death, even Amos Blackiston's, was enough to curb everyone's appetite. Mattie cleared the table while Slim attempted to liven things up by suggesting that the men play a few hands of poker. But a gloomy silence fell over the players. Slim and Charley eventually gave up and found excuses to leave. Omaha, Mattie, and Birch were left, preoccupied by their separate thoughts. Several times, Mattie started to say something to Birch, but then realized that Omaha was still there. She could have asked Omaha to leave them, but the presence of her ranch hand seemed as good an excuse as any to keep silent about her visit to Blackiston.

When a sullen Omaha and weary Birch finally left for the bunkhouse later that night, Mattie felt that her burden was lifted.

She wondered why Birch hadn't asked her where she had been this afternoon since she'd made it obvious that she had to establish an alibi. It must have occurred to him that she'd been lying to the marshal for reasons of her own. But Mattie knew that Birch was discreet and probably hadn't wanted to talk to her in front of Omaha just as she hadn't wanted to reveal her intentions in front of her ranch hands as well.

Mattie extinguished all but one kerosene lamp and headed into her bedroom. As she got ready for bed, she felt a hot fury rise up inside her as she recalled that meeting of a few hours ago. She was certain Amos Blackiston was the man who'd killed Joe. Maybe he wasn't the one who pulled the trigger, but he was responsible—Mattie was as sure of this as she was of the fact that he'd been alive when she left—alive and as venomous as an angry rattler.

Weariness replaced her anger, weighing her down as heavily as a rain-soaked saddle. As she snuffed out the lantern and lay in absolute darkness, Mattie knew that sometime tomorrow she would have to tell Jefferson Birch about her visit with Amos Blackiston.

CHAPTER 9

BIRCH went back to the bunkhouse with Omaha, wondering where Mattie had been that afternoon. He'd lingered a moment at the main house, hoping that Omaha would go on ahead so he could talk to the widow alone. Unfortunately, the ranch hand didn't take the hint and waited patiently while Birch reluctantly caught up. By his unsociable presence, Omaha made it clear that he was unwilling to leave Mattie alone with Birch. Birch suspected that Omaha saw him as a rival for Mattie Quinn's affections, and he didn't dismiss the idea too lightly. Birch admitted to himself that he was attracted to her, and that over the past few days he'd gotten the feeling that she was attracted to him as well.

Birch was sure that his client hadn't killed Amos Blackiston. She wouldn't have hired him to find out the truth if she was going to blow a hole through a suspect and be done with it, but she was hiding something from him. He knew whatever it was must have something to do with Blackiston. She wouldn't have been so willing to lie to the marshal otherwise.

No, Mattie Quinn hadn't killed Blackiston, Birch thought. Someone else killed the cattle baron. There was still Luther Capwell. He hadn't met the man yet, but the descriptions he'd gotten from several people made Luther Capwell appear to be a saint next to Amos Blackiston. Yet this "saint" had founded a "Cattlemen's Association" with Blackiston and seemed to have as little regard for small ranchers as his cohort had.

As Birch analyzed the descriptions of the remaining cattle baron, and remaining suspect in the killing of Blackiston, and perhaps Joe Quinn, he realized that everyone had said that Capwell "appeared" to be harmless. There was always that cloud of hesitancy hanging over this positive description.

Maybe Luther Capwell wasn't as harmless as he was made out to be. Birch might have to investigate some of those rumors about small ranchers who might or might not have been pushed off their ranches by Luther Capwell, but right now he drifted off to sleep, resolving to look into this matter in the morning.

Although he wanted to talk to Mattie Quinn at the start of the day about where she'd been when Blackiston was killed, Birch didn't get a chance. When he got to the dining room with his breakfast, only Charley remained, sopping up the yolk of a fried egg with a chunk of fried bread.

He looked up from his plate and grinned. "You sure stirred things up around here, Birch."

Birch didn't know what to make of Charley. In the past few days that Birch had been here, he couldn't remember hearing two words come out of Charley in the same breath.

Birch shook his head. "That's what I get paid to do. Where's Mrs. Quinn today?"

"Oh, she's out riding today with Slim," Charley said, disapproval dripping from his voice. "There's some fence that needs fixing and they're going to drive a herd in at the end of the day."

"And Omaha?"

"He's in town getting lumber. We got to get that barn rebuilt this week if we're going to drive our cattle into the mining towns within the next few weeks."

"Where do you usually sell your cattle this time of year?"

"Bozeman, Fort Ellis, and towns in that area. We don't usually have to drive too far because we're one of the small outfits. Small outfits cover more ground in a day than, say, Capwell does."

"Who scouts ahead?"

"I do," Charley said. "But this year, we got three hundred head of cattle to drive with half the manpower. There are a few hands from other small ranches in the area who have agreed to help us on this drive," Charley added reluctantly, "but I guess Mrs. Quinn will be coming along anyway."

Birch hazarded a guess. "You don't approve of women out on the range?"

"Womenfolk belong in the kitchen, not out on the range riding fence."

"But don't you think that under the circumstances, Mrs. Quinn has a right to learn that business?" Birch pointed out, then added, "Besides, she has better protection when she's with one of you."

"I guess so," Charley conceded reluctantly. "What's your plan now?"

"I thought I'd go talk to Luther Capwell."

Charley whooped, "That's rich. You and what army?"

"What do you mean?"

Charley explained, "Unless you're known on sight, his guards have orders to shoot to kill." The ranch hand scratched his head and frowned. "Can't understand it, a nice fellow like him."

"Well then, how does a man get to talking to Capwell?"

Charley waved a dismissive hand. "Just hang around Bo's saloon a while. He'll be in."

"He likes to drink?"

The grizzled old ranch hand grunted. "That, and he owns the damn place."

"But it's named after someone named Bo," Birch pointed out.

"Yep, the former owner. He's only the bartender now. Borrowed money from Capwell to buy a shipment of liquor and now Capwell owns the place."

Birch nodded.

Charley leaned over and said, "Some folks around here think you're a hired killer. How many people you killed?"

Birch hesitated, then decided to play along. He might get more out of Charley if the man thought he was a gunfighter.

"I'm not partial to putting notches in my gun. And I don't like to be called a hired killer. Call me a . . . troubleshooter."

Charley stood up, empty plate in his hand. "What's a troubleshooter?"

"When I see trouble, I shoot."

The ranch hand laughed all the way out of the dining room.

After his meal, Birch rode into Rattlesnake. Someone had to know something about Mattie Quinn's troubles. Birch also wanted to talk to the marshal. Maybe this time he could convince the lawman that someone carried a grudge against the Quinns.

The ride into town took about an hour and was uneventful. It was late morning by the time Birch arrived and Rattlesnake was quiet. The ex-Texas Ranger wanted to walk around and get a feel for the town and its inhabitants before talking to the marshal.

He went down to the general store to buy a box of bullets for his Navy Colt and got the impression from the way the bespectacled clerk stared at him that not many strangers passed through Rattlesnake.

"You're not from around here, are you?" the pockmarked-faced shop assistant asked curiously. "You just passing through?"

Birch replied, "Actually, I just got into town a few days ago. I'm working for Mrs. Quinn a few miles out of town."

"Mattie Quinn? Too bad about her husband," the clerk said. "Joe Quinn was a good man. It's hard to believe that he died cleaning his rifle. He was always careful around his Winchester."

Birch asked, "Did you know Quinn well?"

"When I first came out here, I didn't know how to use a rifle. Joe taught me how to shoot and clean one." He shook his head. "I just can't believe it."

He pursued the subject with the bespectacled clerk as

casually as he could manage. "Rumor has it around town that it wasn't an accident. What do you think?"

The man behind the counter suddenly fell silent. Birch watched the clerk's eyes narrow behind his thick wire-rimmed glasses as if he were remembering something important.

Birch prompted the clerk. "I asked you a question, mister."

"I just remembered hearing the marshal say something about the widow Quinn hiring a man who was good with a gun."

Down in Texas, Birch had lived by the code of the gun as well, but his title, Texas Ranger, had commanded a certain respect, nevertheless. Rangers were welcomed in a troubled town by the good citizens who wanted to live in peace. But here in the Northern Territories, there was no equivalent of the Texas Rangers and Birch was just another gunfighter to most folks.

Over the last few years, Birch had learned that without that badge of respect, many people looked at you askance. They didn't trust a man at his word because so many men who swore they were on the right side of the law could turn to the other side in the blink of an eye. He understood their reluctance, but it still made him impatient when someone jumped to conclusions.

"In my line of work," Birch began, "you have to be good with a gun. But that's not the only thing I do. I'm here to ask questions and solve Mrs. Quinn's problems as peacefully as possible. Now, can you tell me anything about Joe's death or what happened afterward?"

The shop assistant looked frightened. He shook his head again. Birch wondered if the fellow had some kind of nervous condition that made him shake his head all the time.

"I can't help you. I really can't." The rush of words stumbled over each other to escape. The clerk backed away from the counter. "Um, you'll have to leave. I'm closing the store for an hour."

As Birch walked out, the timid man called after him, "I really don't know anything. Honestly."

It had to be someone who was still alive who struck such terror in a lowly clerk.

Birch took a chance and asked, "Does Luther Capwell really frighten you that much?"

The clerk's eyes widened. He hesitated, opened his mouth to say something, then appeared to change his mind. "Luther Capwell is a fine man." He started to shut the door, then turned back and said emphatically, "A fine man."

The door was shut firmly in Birch's face.

Birch pulled his hat off to brush away some imaginary dust. He needed a drink, but first he'd have a talk with the marshal.

Marshal Cobb was at his desk fiddling with the jail cell keys. There was only one cell, which seemed enough for a town with a population of less than one hundred. The lawman looked up when Birch approached his desk.

"You come to turn yourself in, Birch?"

"No. I came to ask you if you've learned anything more about Quinn and Blackiston's murders."

Cobb smiled humorlessly. "So now you're tying them together."

Birch replied mildly. "It seems like a possibility."

"I don't deal in possibilities, Birch. Just facts." Marshal Cobb's voice took on a darker tone. "And the fact that you work for Mattie Quinn is interesting. I'm still thinking about it."

"Have you thought about other facts, Marshal? Or do you just ignore them, too?"

"What other facts?" Cobb leaned back in his chair.

"The fact that there was a carved up prize bull on her doorstep a few days ago. Even if you choose to ignore all the other evidence, you can't ignore the message written in blood. And what are you doing about finding Blackiston's killer?"

Cobb was silent for a moment, then replied, "Look, Birch. I'm paid to do a job and if you don't think I'm doing a good enough job, maybe you should wear this badge." Cobb stood up behind his desk. "It just so happens that Blackiston and Capwell had alibis for the day Joe died. Both men were in full sight of their ranch hands the entire day. And now Amos Blackiston is dead, so that kind of lets him out, doesn't it?" After a slight hesitation, he added, "As for Amos Blackiston, I'm still looking into his murder and as I dig deeper, I'm hard-pressed to come up with a better suspect than you or the widow Quinn."

Birch sighed. "Marshal, Capwell is wealthy enough to have hired others to do his dirty work. So was Blackiston. You know that. I think you wouldn't have blinders on if you weren't pocketing that extra pay from the Cattlemen's Association."

Cobb turned red. "No one's ever accused me of favoritism, Birch. You know it's strictly business. There's nothing wrong with a lawman getting paid a little extra for special attention to a saloon or a landowner."

Birch leaned against the lawman's desktop and said calmly, "There's nothing wrong with that if it's not affecting your judgment during a murder investigation."

Marshal Cobb changed the subject. "You thought it was Amos Blackiston behind all of the Quinn troubles. Now that he's dead, where does that leave you?"

Birch had another suspect in mind, but he didn't feel like being cooperative with the lawman today. If Gordy Cobb was going to convince himself that there was nothing wrong in making a few easy dollars, Birch wasn't going to count on the Rattlesnake lawman for anything—and that included finding the real killer or killers of Joe Quinn and Amos Blackiston.

He headed for the saloon. A pot belly stove stood in the middle of the room, emitting the glow of dying embers from earlier this morning. Places like this never closed. Most likely, the bartender slept in the back and the townspeople who came in too late or too early could just help themselves to the red-eye whiskey behind the bar and leave their money in the box under the counter.

Birch called for a whiskey. When the bartender served it up, Birch remarked, "Too bad about Amos Blackiston."

The man behind the bar nodded warily. "Yeah. He was an important man in this town."

"Who do you think did it?"

The bartender squinted perceptibly at Birch. "You're new in this town, ain't you, mister?" A light dawned in his eyes and he answered his own question. "Sure, I remember you. You came into town on the night the Quinn barn burned down. You went out there. I bet you're the hired gun everyone in town's been talking about."

Birch sighed inwardly. He was just about to launch into his explanation of the difference between a hired gun and an investigator when the batwings slapped open on either side. The man who came through them nodded to the bartender, then turned his attention to Birch. His glance took in the ex-Ranger's Colt and seemed to register the fact that Birch was a stranger.

"The usual, Chester?" Birch noticed the bartender's hand wasn't pouring as steadily as before.

Chester grunted and sat a few seats down from Birch. Birch observed Chester from his corner eye, taking in the man's fearsome features. His face was all angles and planes, burned mahogany from outdoor living. Chester might have been a handsome man to the ladies, Birch thought idly, if it weren't for his small eyes and mean mouth.

Another customer staggered through the door, swinging an almost empty whiskey bottle carelessly around. It was hard to tell how old he was. His nose was purple with veins from too much drink and looked ready to explode if you lit a match too close. His uncombed shock of white hair hung over his left eye and his clothes smelled of horse manure. Birch made a wild guess about where this character worked.

"Hey, Bo!" the drunk slurred. "Can you set me up with another bottle? I can pay you on Tuesday."

The bartender shook his head. "Can't, Stinky. You still owe five dollars from last week."

"Aw, I'm good for it," Stinky pleaded. "You know that, Bo."

"You're good-for-nothing, you mean," Chester sneered.

Birch noticed that Bo had fallen silent and concentrated on polishing a spot on the bar. He must have polished that spot many times because it was smooth and worn, almost shiny.

Chester continued with contempt, "Why don't you get out of my sight, you old sot. I get sick from the smell of you."

Stinky just stood there, blinking and swaying. "I just want a drink. Haven't had one since . . ."

Chester threw his empty shot glass at the old man, who cringed as the glass missed and shattered against one of the rough wood walls. Stinky looked down wordlessly at the pieces of shot glass on the floor as if he weren't surprised by this bully's actions. As if it were an everyday occurrence.

"Get out of here, I said. Leave me in peace," Chester shouted at Stinky. He stalked over to the old lush and shoved him in the middle of the chest. Stinky stumbled back through the batwings, landing with a thud on the sidewalk outside.

Birch made the decision to leave before Chester turned his rage on a complete stranger. He'd seen men like Chester before, men who worked themselves into a lather, provoked by nothing at all, belligerent when they were sober—and worse when they were drunk. Although Birch wasn't afraid, he didn't see the point in fighting for no reason. It was easier to walk out the door.

But Chester had other ideas. He stepped in front of the batwings and said, "Where are you going, stranger? That old drunk is fine, I didn't hurt him none. Come have a drink."

Birch replied in his mildest voice, "Thanks, but no thanks." He tried to go around Chester, but the man grabbed him by the sleeve.

"I asked you nice once. I don't like it when someone turns down an invite from me when I'm feeling generous. Now I'm telling you to come have a drink with me."

"You weren't feeling generous a moment ago with that old man," Birch pointed out. "Why don't you call him back in here and buy him a drink?"

"Because I don't feel like it. You and me have some things to discuss."

"Who are you?" Birch asked. Obviously this man had tossed Stinky out on his ear for a reason. Maybe Chester had some information and didn't want anyone around. Birch glanced at Bo, who averted his eyes and pretended to work.

"Who I am is not important. Who you are, is. You're working for Mattie Quinn, aren't you?"

"That's common knowledge. What's your point?"

Chester took a step toward Birch. "I just thought you should know that some people around here would be happier if you moved on."

Birch rubbed his long jaw and, although he didn't feel like it, chuckled. "Let me understand this. Are you threatening me?"

The bully threw his shoulders back and replied, "I wouldn't call it a threat. It's more like some friendly advice."

Although Birch would have liked to learn more about Chester—who he was and who he worked for—it was too tempting to do what he did next.

"Oh? Well, then, let me return the favor." With that, Birch planted a fist in Chester's gut, driving him backward. Chester righted himself and got ready to charge Birch when the batwings creaked.

Could Stinky have come back? Birch dared not look. His attacker lunged for Birch and got him by the shirt, ready to take a swing.

A sharp voice called out, "That's enough, Chester."

Chester looked toward the voice, snarled, and pushed Birch away, retreating into a corner with a bottle and a shot glass.

"I apologize for my cowhand, stranger."

Birch felt a hand on his shoulder, and spun around to face a well-dressed man of medium height. He wore his black hair slicked back gambler-fashion and had bushy eyebrows and long sideburns. His silk brocade vest and black pinstripe suit fit him handsomely.

"Luther Capwell." The man stuck his hand out.

"Jefferson Birch." He took Capwell's hand and shook it.

"Oh, so you're the hired gun out at the widow Quinn's place," Capwell said, a glint of amusement in his eye.

Birch nodded shortly. How could this personable man be the one responsible for all those deaths? But then Birch remembered what Charley had told him about Capwell's ranch being so well-guarded. Capwell might be likable in town but one loco son-of-a-bitch back at his ranch. Birch had met politician-types before and he began to realize Luther Capwell fit the bill perfectly. It all started to make sense.

"I work for Mattie Quinn," Birch admitted. "And if you're not busy at the moment, maybe I could ask you a few questions."

Capwell's amused expression darkened. "What kind of questions?"

"What is your interest in the Quinn land? You offered to buy the land a few months ago."

Capwell smiled politely and replied, "My interest is in acquiring more land."

Birch persisted. "But as I understand it, their land doesn't border yours."

Capwell nodded. "That's true, but you may be aware of the Montana Cattlemen's Association. I'm one of the founding members, as was Amos Blackiston, may he rest in peace." The cattle baron continued, "We've made no secret of our goal to buy out all of the small ranchers and create several large spreads."

"Why?"

"To control the price of cattle," Capwell said, beaming. "It was my idea, of course. My father is a merchant and taught me that if the competition is narrowed down to only a few, profits increase."

Birch asked bluntly, "Did you kill Bláckiston in an effort to watch your profits grow?"

Capwell's smile was hard. "If I did, do you think I'd admit it to you, Mr. Birch? I think our conversation has ended." He started to walk toward the bartender and Birch tried to follow, but Chester had moved between them. Bo was keeping an eye on Birch as well. The ex-Texas Ranger realized that the odds were against him. He left the saloon.

As he turned to walk down the street toward Cactus, he heard, "Psst! Hey, stranger."

Stinky was standing in the entrance to an alley next to the saloon, motioning to Birch. Birch moved closer, downwind from the furtive old man.

"I heard you're looking for information," Stinky said in a low voice. "I just might have something you'd be interested in."

"Okay," Birch replied. "But I get the feeling that you want something for your trouble."

Stinky grinned, exposing a toothless maw. "A feller's gotta make money somehow around here."

"How much?" Birch dug his hand into his pocket.

"Oh, two dollars will be enough." Stinky reached out to take the silver dollars, adding, "But you'll have to meet me back here tonight for the information."

Birch gave him only one of the dollars.

"Hey!" Stinky growled.

Holding up the other silver dollar, Birch smiled coolly and said, "You'll get this one tonight when you meet me."

He turned to walk away and noticed that Chester was standing outside the saloon, staring in his direction.

CHAPTER 10

BIRCH stayed in town for supper. He was suddenly weary of all the riding back and forth. Back in the saloon, Birch ordered his meal. It was just about dark and he knew he had to meet Stinky in the alley soon, but he didn't like the idea. He had a nagging feeling that something was about to go wrong.

Luther Capwell and his trained dog Chester had already gone, and the saloon continued to be more empty than full. There was only one meal being served by the bartender and it was a poor one at that, consisting of beans, bacon, and hard crusty bread with a whiskey to wash it all down. It was filling but tasteless, and Birch noticed that most of the men who came in ordered beer or whiskey, not a meal.

Birch half-expected Stinky to wander in again, looking to buy another bottle. But he didn't show. Maybe he figured he'd better stay away until after the meeting. As soon as darkness fell, Birch put his whiskey bottle aside and left the saloon.

Rattlesnake remained quiet, even after dark, but there were quite a few folks out for a small town. The bespectacled pockmarked-faced clerk from the general store passed by with a woman who, from her no-nonsense look, was probably his wife.

Birth crossed the street to get a better view of the alley where Stinky was supposed to meet him. For the next half an hour, people walked by, young couples courting or sober men determined not to stay sober. Birch began to think that the whole Rattlesnake population was out for a walk or heading for the saloon.

And all that time, Birch didn't see one sign of Stinky. He started to worry. Maybe the old man was watching the alley to see if Birch would show.

When the street was empty, Birch stepped out from the shadows and crossed the street to the alley. He heard voices coming from a distance, maybe somewhere down the street. Birch stayed back in the alley to allow them to pass without seeing him. Another courting couple walked by, too caught up in each other to notice Birch lurking in the shadows.

Taking a step backward, Birch stumbled on something crumpled up across the alley. He bent down and touched flesh. A familiar smell wafted past his nose. Even in the darkness of the alley, he knew it was Stinky.

As Birch's eyes adjusted to the darkness, he could make out something around the old man's neck. Peering closer, he realized that it wasn't something on the dead man's neck—a knife had sliced a gash across his throat.

Birch shuddered. It looked like a horrible way to die. He guessed that Stinky had been like this for several hours, probably having had his throat cut while Birch was taking his meal in the saloon.

The rumbling voices of approaching men caught Birch's attention. He stood up and bent nearer to the entrance of the alley, then slipped out of the alley and headed for his horse.

Birch took Cactus's reins and led the animal around the side of a building where he had a better view of the arriving men and the alley. There were four of them, including the marshal. They stopped at the alley entrance and two men held their lanterns up to throw a weak light on Stinky's body. Cobb bent over him.

"Yeah, he's dead all right," the marshal said, turning to one of the men. He added, "Nothing you can do, Doc, except fill out the certificate. Maybe you'd better have a look, though."

Birch had already guessed that the doctor was the one

carrying the black leather satchel. The doctor wore mutton-chops and wire-rimmed spectacles, no coat, and his sleeves rolled up as if he'd just gotten out of surgery. He bent over the corpse to examine the throat wound more thoroughly.

Birch turned Cactus around and headed out of Rattle-snake as quietly as possible. As he headed for the ranch, Birch thought back to their surreptitious meeting that after-noon outside the saloon. Stinky had been cautious when he met with Birch, but not cautious enough. Or could it have been Birch's fault?

When he'd finished talking to Stinky, he'd noticed that Chester was standing nearby. Could Chester have overheard them and told somebody else? Or could Chester have been the one who killed Stinky, setting up Birch for the murder by leaving the body in the alleyway and sending an anony-mous message to the marshal, just about the time Birch was supposed to arrive? Or could this all be tied in with the mysterious and apparently well-liked Luther Capwell?

Birch didn't even know exactly what Chester did for Lu-ther Capwell, but he was willing to bet that it wasn't book-keeping. He'd ask Mattie what she knew about him.

Soon he saw the flickering lights of the Quinn main house in the distance. He knew he'd have to talk to Mattie when he got back. He wanted to find out where she'd been when Blackiston was killed.

Birch liked a problem to be simple; this was getting too complicated. At first, it appeared that Amos Blackiston had ordered the murder of Joe Quinn when he wouldn't sell his land. When the widow wouldn't cooperate, Blackiston had some of his men kill her prize bull, write a bloody message on her door, and later burn down her barn. It had all fit together nicely until Amos Blackiston got himself killed.

Mattie Quinn must have heard him coming because she'd opened the door cautiously at first, then wider when she saw who it was. Instead of her usual heavy pants and shirt for outdoors work, she wore a soft blue dress, a simple dress for around the house. But the way it fell flattered Mattie Quinn's figure and the color brought out her dark hair and the blue in her hazel eyes.

The widow Quinn shifted in the doorway as if uncomfortably aware that Birch was staring at her. She lowered her eyes and a soft pink flush warmed her cheeks.

"Good evening, Mr. Birch. We missed each other this morning and you didn't appear for the evening meal. Won't you come in?"

He realized he'd been staring and quickly took his hat off. "Excuse me, Mrs. Quinn. It's just that . . ."

"You've never seen me in a dress before." She stepped aside to let him in. It was warm inside and a pot of coffee sat on the rough-hewn table in the parlor.

He followed her to the table and she poured him some coffee and set it down in front of him.

"I'm sorry if I startled you," she said with a half-smile, fingering her skirt. "It's just that this is—was—Joe's favorite dress and it makes me feel good to put it on some evenings."

Now that they were sitting near a kerosene lamp, he observed telltale red marks around her eyes as if she'd been crying.

"Have you learned anything today?" she asked. "I spent most of today riding with Slim. I try to stay away from working with Charley. He doesn't approve of a woman getting her hands dirty."

"In his own way, I think he's concerned about you," Birch assured her. "I was in town today. A man was murdered and I think it's connected, somehow."

"How awful!" Mattie gasped and her hand flew up to her cheek. "Do you know who it was?"

"I don't know his proper name, but I heard someone refer to him as Stinky." Birch looked uncomfortable. "He was going to sell me some information, but I think someone overheard us talk because a few hours later, he'd had his throat cut."

Mattie nodded, her complexion pale. "I knew him slightly. He used to be a small rancher near the Capwell spread. His land was bought up and he never left the area. His name was Andrew . . . something. I'm not sure. But he worked for the marshal sometimes, and the stables."

And he was about to tell me how Capwell got his land, Birch thought.

He asked, "Can you tell me what you were doing yesterday during the time Blackiston was killed?"

She rubbed her forehead and closed her eyes. "I've been meaning to tell you this . . ." Taking a deep breath, she began. "After I hired you through your agency and you showed up, you didn't look the way I pictured a detective . . ."

Birch looked down to hide a smile. "What did you think I'd look like?"

She tilted her head slightly and said, "Like a banker. Like that Pinkerton fellow." Mattie Quinn continued, "You look more like a man who's good with a gun. And I got to thinking how I could use that to my advantage."

Birch's smile disappeared. "How?"

She said hurriedly, "You have to understand that I meant to bring this whole nightmare to an end. After your visit with Amos Blackiston, I went out there."

"Why didn't I see you on the way back here? You should have passed me."

She shook her head. "I used another trail. I thought that your talk with Blackiston would put a scare into him and he'd be willing to negotiate with me about water rights."

Birch frowned and asked, "How would that help?"

She bit her lip. "I was hoping he'd slip up and say something that would help your investigation."

He stood up, walked over to the fireplace, and said in a voice tight with anger, "In other words, you didn't trust me to investigate on my own."

"No, that's not what I thought at all!" she protested in a harsh, pleading tone. "I only meant to help you. Sometimes a woman can get a man to say things that he wouldn't say to another man. That's all I meant."

"So you told the marshal that you'd seen me out by the barn all afternoon when I returned from my meeting with Blackiston in order to give yourself a cover story as well."

Mattie avoided his eyes and said, "I'm not proud of what I did, but I meant well."

Birch looked into her eyes for a minute, then simply nodded and asked, "Why didn't you just tell me the truth last night?"

Her shoulders slumped wearily and she said without looking at him, "Omaha was here. I didn't want to talk in front of him."

"You weren't seen by anyone else? His wife or daughter, perhaps?"

Mattie shrugged. "Maybe someone saw me, but I only saw Blackiston."

Birch drank some of his coffee and said, "If someone had seen you, Marshal Cobb would be here arresting you right now." After a moment, he asked, "What was Blackiston's mood when you went to see him?"

She sighed and ran a hand through her hair. "He was still angry from your visit. He couldn't understand why I'd hired you." She paused and laughed, but it sounded hollow. "It's all right for him to hire someone to kill my husband, but it's not all right for me to hire you to find out the truth."

Birch said, "The funny thing is that I'm not sure what the truth is anymore."

Mattie looked up sharply. "You don't believe me? Then you do think I killed Amos."

"No, that's not what I said. I believe you. I'm just not sure who's behind all of this," Birch said. "By the way, Mrs. Quinn. I met Luther Capwell in town today. He broke up a fight I was in with a man called Chester."

"Chester? What does he look like?"

Birch described him to her. "Angular face, dark from the

sun, tall and thin. Meanest eyes I ever saw. He was at the saloon this afternoon. Pushed Stinky around and tossed him out on his ear."

Mattie shuddered visibly and ran her hands up and down her arms. "There's a few fellows named Chester around here, but only one who fits your description. His last name's Grundy and he works for the Cattlemen's Association."

A light went on for Birch. "He's the Association detective."

Mattie replied drily, "Gunslinger is a more appropriate term. Chester Grundy is just an outlaw with a fancy title."

"Well, it explains a few things for me." Birch reached over and poured another cup of coffee.

They sat in silence while Birch turned some things over in his head. When the last of the coffee was gone, Birch bid Mattie Quinn good night and went back to the bunkhouse. The sound of ranch hands snoring filled the darkness as Birch lay on his bed, still thinking.

There were so many dead ends. And everything led back to Luther Capwell. Birch knew he had to face Capwell soon, maybe on his own ground, if he could get past the guards.

Birch slept very little that night.

CHAPTER 11

THE men rode out on the range the next morning to round up the cattle. Mattie stayed behind to clear up some business. A barn would have to be built soon or the horses wouldn't have any shelter for the hard winter ahead.

With Amos Blackiston dead, Mattie was beginning to despair that she may never know whether or not Blackiston killed Joe or ordered his death. With the cattle baron in his grave, a hired killer certainly wouldn't admit guilt.

From the way Birch talked last night, it certainly didn't sound like it would be easy for him to get Luther Capwell to talk. And even if he killed Joe Quinn *and* Amos Blackiston, was he likely to confess? Somehow, she doubted it. But who else had a motive to kill both men? Of course, Mattie realized, she was assuming that the murders were tied together, along with the killing of the old drunk in town.

Even with the marshal working on Amos Blackiston's killing and Jefferson Birch working on Joe Quinn's death, Mattie wondered it these investigations would ultimately lead nowhere.

Mattie let out a frustrated sigh. It wasn't fair that Joe had been taken away from her so suddenly.

A rider was approaching, so she took a rifle down from the rack by the door—a reaction that had become automatic since the day Joe died.

Peering out of a window cautiously, she was annoyed to see that the marshal was walking his horse up to her front door. After the way he'd handled the inquiry into Joe's death, she was certain she'd never trust him again.

"State your business, Marshal," she greeted him as she

stepped out of her front door, the shotgun resting in her grip. "What brings you out this way?"

"Uh, morning, Mrs. Quinn," he said, dismounting. "I was on my way out to the Blackiston place and I just thought I'd drop by. Wanted to see how you were doing." He stared at her shotgun pointedly and cleared his throat, repeating, "I thought I'd better see how you were doing here alone in the main house."

"That's mighty decent of you, Marshal," Mattie said, sarcasm dripping from her voice. She gestured to her rifle and added, "I'm doing fine at the moment."

The lawman looked as if he had something else to say, but nothing came of it.

"I sure am sorry about Joe. He was a good fellow."

"Is that all you came out here for?" Mattie asked. She could feel her throat tightening, and when she glanced at her hold on the shotgun she noticed her knuckles were white.

Gordy Cobb took his hat off and averted his eyes. "Aw, look, ma'am. I'm not good at stuff like this, but I have to tell you. There's some rumors around town that you're the leader of a gang of rustlers."

Mattie narrowed her eyes and said, "And I suppose Omaha, Charley, and Slim are the gang, right? Did I start up this gang before or after Joe died?"

"The rustling just began the other day. It goes without saying that I don't believe you or your men are involved."

Mattie couldn't help muttering, "How kind of you."

Cobb went on. "I'm trying to track down who started the rumor, but so far no one seems to know." He looked frustrated and added, "And the fact is that some horses *are* missing from the Capwell ranch. Luther was out to see me earlier today to report it."

Mattie wondered if Amos had started the rumor before he died, but she kept her mouth shut even though she was furious. It wouldn't do well to speak ill of the dead, even if he was a low-down snake-in-the-grass.

"Do you have any idea who might be doing such a thing?"

Cobb scratched his head and replied, "Well, the string of horses was taken from Luther Capwell's place yesterday. The rustlers will make a mistake sooner or later and then I'll be there to bring them in."

"Well we haven't had trouble with rustlers," Mattie said harshly, "but it wouldn't surprise me if we were next in line. Our barn burned down and Joe's prize bull, Old Gumption, was killed and left by my door."

"Look, Mrs. Quinn. You could have come to me with your problems instead of hiring that gun, Birch."

"At least that 'gun,' as you call him," Mattie raised her voice angrily, "believes me and has stood up to the powerful men in this county. Which is more than I can say for the law around here."

Marshal Cobb's brow darkened. "Are you calling me a coward, Mrs. Quinn?"

Mattie felt a cold, trembling anger building up inside. "I didn't use that word, you did. I don't think I'd call a lawman who makes extra money by doing favors for private citizens a 'coward.' I'd just call him a simpleton."

The marshal was silent, but his narrowed eyes and red face said it all. Finally, he managed to croak out, "Chester Grundy may be out here to inspect your horses today or tomorrow. It's nothing to worry about because it's routine when there's been a rustling reported. We check all the ranches in the area. I'll try to accompany him to be sure he won't be making false accusations."

So the only reason Gordy Cobb is here, she thought, is to let me know that I'm in for more of a rough time and there's not a damn thing he's going to do about it.

When she didn't respond, he leaned forward and said in a tone that told her he wasn't sorry at all, "I'm real sorry about the rustling rumors. I've tried to stop them, but you know how some people are when they shoot their mouth off about someone else's dirt."

"Yes, you mentioned that to me before, Marshal."

He appeared to have better control of his anger by now. "And if you have nothing to hide, it would be best for you if you don't put up too much of a fuss about it."

"What a shame that we'll be making it easy for him," Mattie replied drily. "We just started roundup today. He'll be able to check all the horses without having to ride all fifty acres."

CHAPTER 12

TWO-BIT kept a watchful eye on the longhorn cattle grazing nearby as the string of horses drank from the stream. His partner, Jess, had to go back to the Blackiston bunkhouse because he had a bellyache, but he promised to send someone to take his place for the day. Two-Bit suspected that Jess's bellyache came more from a two-bottle hangover than anything else. He'd told Jess more than once that rye shouldn't ought to be mixed with rum.

It felt almost like spring today, but Two-Bit knew from experience that fall was in the air. Soon the trees would turn the color of rust, the leaves stripped away until there were only bare branches. The cold would get colder and snow would cover everything. Pretty soon, Two-Bit would be seeing his breath come out in moist clouds.

He wished someone would show up. Two-Bit got nervous when he was watching one hundred head of cattle by himself. If a calf wandered away, he couldn't go after it without jeopardizing the rest of the herd. And probably worst of all, he couldn't let the string of horses out of his sight for long because horses were a damn sight more valuable than cattle.

When a cow was stolen, it was bad, but cattle could be replaced easily. A good horse was another thing altogether. Without a horse, a cowpuncher couldn't oversee the herd. Couldn't keep up with the longhorns either.

The ranch hand pulled his string of horses away from the stream and tied them to a bush about twenty feet away from the herd. He wished Jess would get back. He was getting thirsty and he couldn't get off his damn horse to fill his canteen without taking his eye away from the herd.

Two-Bit sighed and pulled out his tobacco pouch. A chaw of tobacco would keep his thirst at bay. Reaching inside for a plug, Two-Bit felt only empty space. Damn! he thought, Ab's been in my pouch again.

He felt slightly annoyed with the old hand. Ab used to be a first-rate cowhand before his joints froze up. Now he just cooked the meals. The old man had always been partial to Two-Bit, since he was the youngest cowpunch, but sometimes Abner took a little too much liberty with Two-Bit's tobacco pouch. Why, Ab was the fellow who gave Two-Bit his nickname. Said it was because he was always asking to borrow two bits until pay day.

Meanwhile, Two-Bit was without his tobacco and was mighty thirsty. He kept an eye out for some sign that one of the fellows back at the main house might be along, but after a few minutes, he realized that Jess had probably just fallen into his bunk without letting anyone know that he was alone. It might be hours before anyone realized that he was riding herd by himself.

The young cowpuncher sighed and assessed the situation. It wouldn't be the first time a lone hand abandoned his herd for a few minutes to go behind some bushes or to fill up his canteen. And what could happen in a few minutes? He would still be in hearing distance so if any rustler tried to steal the string, he would be on him like a fly on molasses. Besides, he thought as he looked around, he was all alone.

Comforted by this thought, Two-Bit steered his horse toward the clear stream. He dismounted and pulled his canteen off his saddle. After filling it up, he stooped down and took a few big gulps to relieve his immediate thirst, pulling back and wiping his mouth with his sleeve.

That didn't take long, Two-Bit thought with satisfaction as he mounted his roan. Now I'll be set until one of the boys shows up.

His eye roamed over the peacefully grazing longhorns. Occasionally one bull would nudge another bull with those long pointy horns and there'd be a slight scuffle, but all in all, Two-Bit had to admit that it was a pretty peaceful setting. He sat and enjoyed the tranquility for some time, until he heard the sound of hoofbeats and turned to see another ranch hand riding toward him.

"Hey, Two-Bit," Stu greeted, "has it been quiet? We found Jess passed out on his bunk about an hour ago and I rode on out here."

Two-Bit grinned. "You know it has. Nothing ever happens here on the range."

Stu looked around. "Where's the string? Shouldn't they be tied up somewhere where you can keep an eye on them?"

Two-Bit caught his breath. He hadn't even looked in that direction since coming back from filling his canteen. Could they have gotten loose somehow and wandered off?

Two-Bit turned around without a word and rode off a distance, hoping that the horses had just wandered off to graze beyond the copse. The range stretched as far as the eye could see and there was no sign of them.

Stu's voice came from behind Two-Bit, angry and hard. "Well, that's just great, Two-Bit. Not one damn horse beyond the two cayuses we're sittin' on right now. Damn it, boy, what were you doin' back here all alone?"

"I just went to the stream to fill my canteen," Two-Bit tried to explain. He was already having visions of being told to pack his things tonight and move on. He didn't even own a horse. He'd have to carry his saddle into town, maybe sleep out under the stars just outside of town. "I don't know how this could have happened. I . . . "

Stu sighed. "It's them clever rustlers. They been to the Capwells', too. I heard around town that the head of the ring is that Quinn woman."

"Joe Quinn's widow? That don't seem right."

Stu leaned forward and said in a low voice, "How do you think she keeps that ranch going? She don't have no more than three hundred head of cattle, if even that. And besides that, she's running the ranch." Stu added darkly, "Women don't have a head for business, but they sure can get into a lot of trouble."

"They can?"

"Yup. Look at Belle Starr and Rose of Cimarron. And what about Cattle Kate?" Stu looked around impatiently.

"What are we going to do, Stu? I guess I'll get my walking papers."

"Aw, who's going to let you go? Mrs. Blackiston? Her daughter Mabel?" Stu reached over and clapped a companionable hand on his partner's shoulder. "Don't worry, we'll get those horses back. They've got the Blackiston brand on them. Let's get these cattle back to the ranch and report the missing horses to the marshal."

As they spurred the cattle on toward the ranch, Two-Bit felt much better. He felt bad about losing that string of horses, but at least he still had a job.

CHAPTER 13

JEFFERSON Birch was at Mattie's side the next day when Chester Grundy rode up. The grim-faced Marshal Cobb accompanied him. News had already traveled to the Quinn property about the stolen Blackiston horses as well.

Grundy didn't bother to dismount, but he faced Mattie Quinn, his cold eyes insolently studying her figure. He tipped his hat to her and said, "I've come to inspect your horses."

Mattie Quinn crossed her arms in a defiant gesture and replied, "Go ahead. All the cayuses have the Quinn brand on them. You won't find any Blackiston horses here. Or Capwell's, for that matter."

Cobb looked around. "Where are your cowhands?"

"Slim's off in the northermost pasture to check on a loose cow, and Charley and Omaha," she gestured beyond the back of the house where the barn should be if they could see it, "have started work on the barn." Sure enough, hammers could be heard in the distance.

Cobb nodded with satisfaction and signalled to Grundy that he should go.

"I'll go with you," Birch offered, starting for his horse.

Grundy looked at Cobb and shook his head.

"Can't let you go, Birch," Cobb said. "We made an agreement that he'd search the grounds and I'd keep an eye on everyone here."

"Slim isn't here, either. What difference does it make if Mr. Birch accompanies him? They'd waste less time," Mattie said, exasperated.

"It would take too much time to track down Slim, but if he

isn't where you say he is, there'll be questions. As for Birch, how could we trust him?"

"Well, why do you need to watch us? Couldn't you go with him?" Mattie asked the marshal.

"Can't do that either. If you did steal the horses, you might try to get away while we're out looking," he reasoned.

The marshal kept his eyes averted as Grundy began his search, riding off to the farthest pasture in the northeast corner of the Quinn property. When he was out of sight, Marshal Cobb turned to Mattie Quinn and said stiffly, "I had no choice. He's with the Association and has the right to request an inspection if he suspects someone of stealing from Association members."

Mattie's expression remained hard as stone. "I'm sure you didn't."

While Cobb and Mattie continued to glare at each other in uncomfortable silence, Birch prowled around the boundaries of the main house restlessly. He should have gone with Grundy. He didn't trust him. What was Grundy's purpose in coming here?

Most of the morning was gone before Grundy returned, a smug glint in his eyes, a mean smile on his sharp face, and ten horses trailing behind him. Slim brought up the caravan, a sheepish expression on his weathered baby face. Grundy and Slim were dismounting just as Mattie and the marshal stepped outside.

Mattie's eyes grew wide with disbelief at the sight of the horses. Then she turned her expression on Birch and shook her head slightly.

"Found these critters wandering around in one of the far pastures by the creek." Grundy couldn't keep the exhilaration out of his voice. He patted the flank of the first horse in the string and added, "If you'll check the earmarks, Cobb, you'll find that they're Capwell stock." He turned his terrible eyes on Mattie. "Looks like those rumors were true. Mattie Quinn is a horse thief."

She opened her mouth to say something, hesitated, then said, "Marshal, I've never seen those horses before. Why, we hardly ever use the corrals way off to the north."

Birch addressed Grundy. "How do we know that you didn't put those horses there yourself?"

"Because I was with him when he found 'em," Slim interjected, carefully avoiding his employer's gaze. He finally looked up briefly and said, "Sorry, Mrs. Quinn. If I'd have known what he was doing, I wouldn't have gone with him and seen the horses with my own two eyes." He shook his head.

Birch turned to Marshal Cobb and said, "Just because the horses were found on her property doesn't mean she's the thief. You heard what she said—those pastures on the edge of her land weren't used much. Anyone who lives around here could have known about them."

Marshal Cobb looked grimly at the other two men, then Mattie. "I'll keep that in mind, Birch. But in the meantime, I'll have to place Mrs. Quinn under arrest."

Birch opened his mouth to protest, but Slim spoke first. "Look, if you gotta arrest her, you might as well arrest me, Omaha, and Charley as well. You don't think she could go stealing horses on her own, do you?"

Grundy grinned. "Seems reasonable to me, Marshal. Why don't you bring 'em all in?"

The marshal looked reluctant. "I don't think there's any need, Chester."

Grundy frowned, obviously not pleased with the marshal's decision. He began, "But Marshal, it's obvious . . . "

Cobb cut in. "It's not obvious to me. She's a widow. I don't believe she's a horse thief any more than most of the people in Rattlesnake will believe it. There's no law anywhere that says I have to take in everyone on this ranch."

Grundy's eyes darkened and he said grimly, "Mr. Capwell's not going to be pleased that you're letting these members of her gang stay free."

Birch watched Cobb's face. A muscle twitched in his jaw. Finally, he said, "I'm the law around here, Grundy. If Mr. Capwell doesn't like it, let him write to the sheriff of this territory."

Cobb turned to Slim and said, "Tell the others what happened. Just don't leave the area."

Grundy spoke. "Marshal, you're making a mistake."

The lawman looked at Grundy and said in a stern voice, "When you're marshal, Chester, you can make the decisions. Until then, you stay out of my way."

Mattie turned to Grundy and said, "Get off my property now. And don't come back."

Grundy replied, "I might have to, ma'am, if I have reason to suspect that you're still stealing horses."

She said with dignity, "How can I? I'll be sitting in a jail cell. But then, you'll be able to figure out some way to blame me for that, too. You know very well I didn't do this."

Birch finally spoke. "I noticed that you only found Capwell's horses. Where are the others?"

Mattie answered with bitterness. "I'm sure they're being well taken care of on Capwell's ranch."

Grundy's smile turned into a frown. "You'd better be careful who you point a finger at, Mrs. Quinn."

"What do I have to lose? You've taken away my freedom and," Mattie hesitated before going on, "you're trying to take away my home as well."

Birch watched in admiration as she stared at Grundy intensely.

"I'll be back later to look for the other horses," Grundy told Cobb as he mounted his horse and led the string of purloined horses away.

After a moment, Birch helped Mattie Quinn up on Slim's horse. Before Cobb led his prisoner away, he turned to Birch and said, "If you can find out anything about all this, I'd suggest that you do it fast. Ranchers don't take too kindly to horse thieves. It's a worse crime than killing a man."

Birch stated, "You don't believe she's guilty either."

Cobb shook his head and said, "But it's out of my hands now. She'll be able to speak her piece when the circuit judge comes around, but I can't promise that it'll be enough."

With that, Cobb and Mattie Quinn headed for Rattlesnake and a jail cell.

Birch ran his fingers roughly through his hair. Now he wished Grundy were still here so he could take a swing at that smug face of his.

"You okay, Birch?" Slim, who stood nearby, asked. "I know just how you feel. It don't seem fair, a pretty woman like that in jail."

Birch growled, "She's innocent, Slim. We all know that."

There was a pause before Slim said, "Yes. I'm sure she is."

CHAPTER 14

BIRCH had stayed back at the main house in case unfriendly visitors decided to take their frustrations out on the Quinn homestead. Slim told his fellow ranch hands the bad news.

Charley kept shaking his head and saying, "That jackass of a marshal. Gordy Cobb oughta be ashamed of himself for putting a young widow through all of this."

Omaha's expression looked like it had been chiseled in granite when he heard about Chester Grundy's visit and Mattie Quinn's arrest.

"How could you stand by and let Gordy Cobb take her away, Birch?" Omaha exploded, pacing back and forth in front of the former Ranger. "If I'd been here . . . "

Charley spoke up. "You'd have gotten yourself arrested along with Mrs. Quinn, you dang fool. There wasn't much he could do with a string of Capwell horses on her property."

Birch took his hat off and scratched his forehead. "Cobb did say that Mrs. Quinn is better off in his jail. There will be ranchers who will blame her for every missing animal in the territory. They might even want to string her up without waiting for the circuit judge to come around."

Omaha continued to pace around the clearing, stopping occasionally to glance at the front door of the main house as if he still saw the bloody message written there above the mutilated bull. Slim rested a foot on the stump where Joe Quinn had been sitting when he was killed a few months back.

Birch watched the cowhands closely, then asked, "Did any of you hear anything last night? Did you see anything unusual yesterday when you were rounding up? What about that pasture—did any of you go out there yesterday?

Omaha looked up sharply and said with obvious annoyance, "Hear anything? No. And I don't think any of us were around that pasture since last week." The other ranch hands concurred. "We rounded up the herd that was in it. There was no reason to go back there this week."

"Capwell's horses were stolen two days ago. Blackiston's yesterday. Why weren't Blackiston's horses found there also?" Birch said, mostly to himself.

Omaha added, "Why couldn't Grundy have planted the horses there when he went looking for them today?"

Slim spoke up. "I would have seen him do it. I just happened to be looking for a runaway steer in that pasture when I caught sight of Grundy. He explained what he was doing, but I didn't trust him, so I rode along with him."

Charley leaned against the horse railing and looked uneasily at his peers. "They can't hang a woman, can they? I mean, it's just not done."

Birch glanced at him and shrugged. "I'm afraid it's been done before. Have you ever heard of Ella Watson?"

Both Charley and Slim frowned, then shook their heads.

"Wasn't she known as Cattle Kate?" Omaha asked.

Birch nodded in acknowledgment, then continued. "There was never any evidence to prove that she was a rustler. In fact, some folks say that one of the ranchers got greedy and started the rumor, then hanged her along with another rancher. The rancher's defense was that some of his cattle had been rustled by Ella Watson."

"How long ago did this happen?" Slim asked.

Birch paused, then said, "A few years ago. I was in the area right after it happened. Folks were still talking about it. As far as I know, the men who killed Ella Watson were never brought to trial."

There was a short silence as the four men contemplated the story just told.

RUSTLER'S VENOM ■ 97

"What needs to be done?" Omaha finally asked Birch.

"I'm going out to the Blackiston ranch again. Maybe their horses have been found. I'm going to talk to the widow."

"I'll go with you," Slim offered eagerly.

"Thanks, but I'd rather go alone. I don't want Mrs. Blackiston or any of her ranch hands thinking I'm there for revenge." Birch walked over to Cactus, took the reins, and mounted his saddle.

"What are we supposed to do in the meantime, Birch?" Omaha asked in an angry tone.

"Go about your business but stay close to the main house. Keep an eye out for trouble that might be headed this way." Birch pointed his horse toward Blackiston's property.

Charley scratched his day's growth and replied, "We'll be here working on the barn and keeping our shotguns nearby."

The hands moved slowly toward the burnt-out site as Birch rode off.

The Blackiston place hadn't changed much on the outside with the exception of a swath of black cloth draped above the door. No guard stepped out to greet Birch with a shotgun hanging from his hand and no young girl stepped lightly across the clearing to greet her father after her ride.

An older version of Mabel Blackiston in a somber black dress opened the door. It was obvious that Mrs. Blackiston had once been as attractive as her daughter, but the years had added creases and fine lines to her face. Her hair was no longer a brilliant auburn like Mabel's, having dulled to a medium brown. While she was no longer pretty, many would still think of her as handsome. Birch wondered how many years she had aged after finding out that her husband had been murdered.

"What can I do for you?" Mrs. Blackiston asked, the grief painfully evident in her eyes.

Birch took his hat off and introduced himself. "My deepest condolences, Mrs. Blackiston. My name is Jefferson Birch."

There was an almost imperceptible change in her demeanor when he said his name. She straightened her shoulders slightly and said stonily, "You're the man who came out to talk to my husband a few hours before he was killed." She narrowed her eyes. "Your visit upset him quite a bit."

"I came here yesterday looking for information from your husband, Mrs. Blackiston." He hated lying, but tried to think of his next words as a stretch of the truth. "He didn't get a chance to tell me everything about his involvement with the Quinn ranch incident. I thought maybe you could help me fill in some gaps."

The widow Blackiston narrowed her eyes and replied, "I remember now. You work for that widow woman, Mattie Quinn—the one whose husband shot himself accidentally. And she went around accusing my Amos of murder afterwards."

Birch shifted from one foot to the other and explained, "I'm just here to find out the truth, ma'am. There's some question as to whether Joe Quinn's death was an accident."

The woman's face remained impassive, but her voice cracked when she replied, "Well, I don't know if Joe Quinn's death was an accident, but I do know that Amos was murdered. And there's been some whispers around here that Mattie Quinn was seen around here not too long before that."

Birch started to reassure the widow. "Mrs. Blackiston, Mattie Quinn didn't do it. If it would be all right, I'd like to . . . "

Her sharp voice cut in. "I'm sorry, Mr. Birch, but I never interfered with my husband's business. You came all the way out here for nothing. Please leave now. I can't help you." She shut the door without waiting for Birch to finish his sentence.

Birch turned to find Mabel Blackiston studying him silently. Aware that this young girl's father had just died, Birch decided against trying to talk to her. She probably didn't know anything about her father's business dealings anyway.

He headed for his horse, Cactus, feeling frustrated in his futile attempts to uncover the truth of the murders.

"What are you doing here?" Mabel called out as she came closer. "I remember you. You were here just before Papa was killed."

"That's right," Birch said, jamming his hat back on his head.

She said, "Papa was very upset when you left."

All Birch could think of to say was, "I'm sorry about your father, Miss Blackiston."

"Thank you for your kind words," Mabel said sarcastically, crossing in front of him to run her hand down Cactus's sleek neck. "The marshal was here again his morning. He mentioned your name on his list of suspects in my papa's murder."

Birch looked down, clearly uncomfortable now. He replied, "I'm sure the marshal considers me a suspect in your father's death, but I left your property directly after you came back from your ride." He rubbed his jaw in remembrance.

She looked up at him with a small smile. "You fought with Wiley before you left the ranch."

He smiled back in concession, realizing that she was too naive to know that her father ordered Wiley to teach him a lesson. "I remember seeing the library curtains move," he admitted, "and wondered if that was your father or you watching."

"Papa went into the kitchen to get another bottle of whiskey after you left." She hesitated before saying, "I know he wasn't considered a very nice man by most of the townfolk and the other ranchers." She cocked her head. "What did you come here for today, Mr. Birch? I know you didn't ride all the way up here just to offer words of sympathy to a grieving widow and her daughter."

Birch couldn't help asking, "Why are you even talking to

me, Miss Blackiston? You of all people should have ordered your ranch hands to escort me off your property by now."

Mabel Blackiston replied quietly, "I've met Mattie Quinn. I don't think she could kill a man, even someone who was threatening her." Mabel evidently read the expression on Birch's face because she added, "I know what you're thinking—you're surprised that I'm aware of my father's business dealings." She shook her head sadly. "I've known about Papa ever since Andy."

Birch blinked and tried not to show the surprise in his voice when he asked, "Andy?"

"He was a young man who began to court me, but Papa didn't like him because he was the son of a small rancher. Papa called him the son of a dirt farmer. My father started rumors, similar to the ones about Mattie Quinn, that eventually ran Andy and his family out of the territory."

Birch asked, "Do you think he could have started the rumors about Mrs. Quinn?"

"No," she answered. "I don't think he'd use the same story twice. He never has before."

"He's done this before?"

Mabel nodded. "Oh yes. I'd overhear him talking to Mr. Grundy," she made a face when she mentioned his name, "and they'd be laughing about the rumors. And Papa didn't run Andy's family off just because of me. He also wanted them off their property for the land and the water rights."

"And I assume he got them."

She looked up with a small smile of triumph. "No. As a matter of fact, Joe and Mattie Quinn ended up with that land. You see, my papa got real sick about then and the doctor ordered him to stay put for a few weeks. And during his illness, the Quinns picked up the land. Papa hadn't been worried about anyone in the area trying to lay claim to the property because everyone knew who was going to get it, but he hadn't counted on strangers moving in."

Birch frowned. So there had been a history of problems

with the Quinn land. He turned to her again. "Mabel, what about Luther Capwell? How does he fit into all of this? He has lots of cattle and a big spread, almost as big as your father's, from what little I know. Would he have any reason to kill Joe Quinn and turn against your father?"

Mabel shuddered and said, "That's always a possibility. My father trusted Capwell because they'd started the Cattlemen's Association together. In fact, Papa was pushing me to be nice to Mr. Capwell. I think he wanted me to marry him."

Suddenly, Mabel looked so young and vulnerable that if Amos Blackiston had been standing there, Birch would have felt like punching him. What kind of father would manipulate his daughter's affections just to make a good business deal? It sounded like a sickness, like gold fever.

Mabel added, "In my opinion, Luther Capwell is not to be trusted."

"Could anyone else working on your ranch have known about your father's practices?"

She shook her head. "I don't think so."

"And you really did lose a string of horses the other day."

"Yes. Two-Bit was supposed to be watching them. He was alone and . . . " she paused and shook her head, "not very reliable, I'm afraid."

"What's he doing here?" someone asked. Birch turned to see Wiley striding over to them, his fists ready to go into action.

Mabel addressed her ranch hand. "I'm talking to him. He had a few questions and . . . "

Wiley growled, "I wouldn't cooperate with him, Miss Blackiston. He may be the one who killed your daddy. Why should any of us help him?" Wiley spat on the ground for emphasis.

Mabel replied, "Mattie Quinn has been arrested, accused of stealing Capwell's horses. And, very possibly, our missing horses."

Birch watched Wiley's face for a trace of a guilty expression. Instead, his face crumpled into a puzzled frown.

The ex-Texas Ranger asked, "How did that string of horses disappear from under your noses? Any chance that one of your hands could have done it?"

Wiley ran a hand across the back of his thick neck. "Well, the horses disappeared because the damn fool cowboy who was supposed to be watching them went to the river to fill up his water bag and didn't think to take the string with him." Wiley shook his head at the young cowpuncher's stupidity. "It never occurred to him that the horses might not mind going down to the river for some water themselves. Two-Bit's not bright enough to do it. He'd need help, but I don't believe any of our hands did it."

Wiley paused, then added, "As to who did it, your guess is as good as mine. For my money, I'd consider Luther Capwell. But I heard some of his horses were rustled the other day."

Birch said, "His horses were the ones found on Mattie Quinn's land. That's why she's in jail."

Wiley had no more information, and he seemed genuinely remorseful that Mattie Quinn had been arrested. Mabel walked Birch back to his horse.

"Thank you, Miss Blackiston, for your help." He tipped his hat to her before mounting Cactus.

"Let me know if there's anything else that can be done." She looked serious for a moment as she said, "Last year, the marshal caught a couple of horse thieves who were driving the horses over the border and selling them in Wyoming Territory."

Mabel Blackiston hesitated, then asked, "They won't hang her, will they?"

Birch said, "I don't know."

CHAPTER 15

GORDY Cobb had just sat down to a strong, hot cup of coffee when the Collins boy burst breathlessly into his office.

"Marshal, you got to come quick!"

Cobb put down his tin mug and said, "Calm down, Nat. Tell me what's happened."

Nat Collins, a gangly fourteen-year-old with a shock of mussed-up yellow hair, took a deep breath and said, "Pa and me found some horses missing."

"When?" The lawman's question came out sharper than he'd intended it to, but Nat took no notice.

"A couple of hours ago. We'd left them down in one of the far pastures this morning, and now they're gone." The boy bit his lip thoughtfully. "Pa's not sure how we're going to get our cattle to market now with five of our horses gone."

Cobb came out from around his desk and squeezed Nat's shoulder. "Let's go, son. We'll look into it."

Before they left, Cobb found Gimpy Higgins down at the stables and instructed him to get over to the jailhouse and watch over Mattie Quinn. So far, there hadn't been a mob scene, maybe because the accused rustler was a woman, and a widow as well. But Cobb couldn't tell when some drunk son-of-a-bitch might whip the crowd at the local saloon into a frenzy over a few missing horses. After tossing down shots of red-eye for an hour, most men could be convinced to do most anything.

The Collins ranch wasn't far out of town—a small place with a hundred or so head of cattle. Matthew Collins and his family worked hard to keep their place. Matt Collins was dark and stocky, but muscular from working the cattle all year long. Patrick, who took after his father in build and coloring, was barely sixteen. In all probability, Nat had been sent to fetch the marshal while Matthew and Patrick searched their fifty acres for traces of the horse thieves.

Kate Collins was a willowy blond with porcelain features. She was waiting just inside the house when Nat arrived with Cobb in tow.

"Come in, Marshal. Matthew and Patrick will be back soon."

"Thank you, Mrs. Collins, but if you can tell me where they might be, I should try to catch up with them. They might have found some trace of the thieves by now."

She shook her head. "I don't know where they could be right now. I know we don't have a large ranch, but it's too big for me to guess where they are."

Nat spoke up. "Marshal, I think I could find them for you."

Nat's mother looked skeptical, but Cobb nodded and said, "Lead on, boy."

Less than an hour later, Nat was shouting and waving his hands at two tiny figures in the distance. The boy had led Cobb up and down several low hills covered with stubby scrub brush and occasional clumps of trees. Cobb could tell that cattle had recently grazed over most of the area they covered in search of Nat's father and brother; if hardy new grass wasn't already growing, the range was bare, dry, and thirsty, waiting for some rain to fall.

When Cobb finally reached the rest of the family, Matt Collins looked angry as hell and Patrick just looked worried. Everyone dismounted to stretch their legs and give the horses a rest.

"What happened, Matthew?"

Collins explained, "I had to go fix a fence about a mile from where the horses were grazing. Patrick and Nat were supposed to watch the horses and the cattle, but it's really just too much to handle for two boys."

Patrick cut in, "We could have handled it if Nat hadn't let that rogue calf get away."

Nat's cheeks flushed and he glared at his older brother.

Matthew Collins reached out and put his hands on both boys' shoulders. "Now, I want both of you to remember that there's no blame here. It could have happened just as easily if all three of us were watching the herd. There just aren't enough of us and somebody must have known that."

Both boys avoided looking at each other.

Cobb nodded and said, "Yeah, it happened to a cowhand on the Blackiston ranch a few days ago. He was left in charge of the herd and a string of horses, and he went down to the river—not more than a hundred yards away—to get some water for himself. When he got back, the cattle were still there and it took another hour or so for him to realize that the horses were gone."

The boys looked up at the lawman with interest. Patrick leaned forward and asked, "What happened? Did you catch the dirty bastard?"

"Patrick!" his father said sharply. "Don't go using language like that. You might slip and use it around your ma someday. You know how damned strict she is about foul language."

"Yes, Pa." Patrick sat back, humbled by his father's warning.

Cobb couldn't help but notice how delighted Nat looked that his big brother had gotten reprimanded.

The lawman cleared his throat and said, "I guess you haven't heard then. Chester Grundy found the Capwell horses on the Quinn property and Mattie Quinn was arrested."

Collins raised his eyebrows and said, "The widow Quinn? I find that hard to believe. Joe and Mattie are good folks. Still, I suppose you never can tell. She was running the ranch after he died and maybe things weren't going so good . . . "

Cobb replied, "Well, she couldn't possibly have stolen your

horses since I've had her locked up since late morning and you claim your horses were stolen just a few hours ago."

Nat asked, "Are you going to let Mrs. Quinn go then, Marshal?"

Cobb shook his head. "She's being held on other charges as well, son. I'm looking into Amos Blackiston's murder."

Matthew Collins's face hardened. "If I weren't a Christian man, Marshal, I'd say that whoever killed him did us all a favor. But I can't believe that Mattie Quinn killed him."

Gordy Cobb felt his jaw tighten. The scene he'd had with the widow Quinn back on her ranch the other day flashed into his mind. Her bitter words rang in his ears. A feeling he'd been unfamiliar with up until a few days ago gnawed at his gut—guilt. Every word Mattie Quinn had said was true.

Gordy Cobb had let himself be blinded by Blackiston and Capwell's money. He'd made it convenient for the two cattle barons to step on people: Andy Faraday and his family had been driven from their land by Blackiston; Lester "Stinky" Crabtree ended up sweeping out the stables in town—and eventually was killed—while Luther Capwell added the Crabtree property to his acreage; and now Joe Quinn was dead and his widow was in jail, accused of rustling horses. And Gordy Cobb had let it happen by standing by and doing nothing.

He nodded to Matthew Collins and replied, "I don't think the Quinn woman is guilty, either." He looked around at the Collins family and said, "Well, let's split up and cover the rest of your property before it gets dark. Maybe we'll have some luck."

They mounted their horses and rode off in different directions.

CHAPTER 16

ELMER Chase was on his way to Rattlesnake to buy some fence wire at the general store when he met the thin man with the mean eyes leading a string of horses, five in all. There was something about the stranger that made Elmer uncomfortable, but if he'd been asked to pin down that feeling, Elmer wouldn't know how to describe it.

To start out, Elmer had been in a bad mood all day. It just seemed like a wasted day to him to have to ride all the way down to Rattlesnake just to pick up some fence wire. True, Elmer needed the fence wire to keep his cattle from wandering, but his neighbor, Prentice Malone, had promised to pick it up when he made a trip down here from nearby Wolf Creek the other day. But old Prent just done and forgot it.

But that's what I get for relying on a senile old man, Elmer thought with disgust. The only person I can rely on is myself.

He had just crossed Rattler Creek and was about twenty miles from Rattlesnake. It was midafternoon and the day was starting to cool off. With autumn in the air, the days got shorter as they got up on the cattle drive season. It had been a fairly dry summer and Elmer was taking in the distant sight of brown and purple hills when he came across the stranger with the horses.

He was dressed in a buckskin shirt and denims with a black hat shading his eyes. From the direction he was going, it looked like he had led the horses to a river a few miles to the northwest and was now getting back on the road to town.

"Howdy, stranger," Elmer greeted. "You heading for Rattlesnake?"

The man slowed down, but didn't stop. His voice was low

and menacing as he replied, "Don't see that it's any business of yours, one way or the other."

Elmer noticed that the stranger's hand rested lightly on the gun at his side, and when the man lifted his head just a little to speak Elmer got a good look at those mean eyes for the first time. They were eyes as full of warmth as a rattlesnake about to strike his victim.

Elmer Chase was no fool. He knew killer eyes when he saw them, unlike some folk. Some men were just too stupid or too proud to make the right move. In the case of such a man, they would look into those venomous eyes and, in a burst of bravado, would say something that would spur this stranger into deadly action.

However, Elmer Chase was not such a man. He had no need to prove himself and, in fact, went out of his way to keep from being on the wrong end of a gun. In this case, Elmer smiled at the stranger and said, "You're right. It ain't any of my business. See, what I really meant to ask was, well, if you were going to Rattlesnake, maybe you were in the mood for a little company. Then I'd have ridden alongside you. I ain't seen a soul all day."

Under other circumstances Elmer would have mentioned what fine horses the stranger had with him, and maybe asked where he'd gotten them, but a small voice inside told him to hold his tongue. The stranger's horses were acting a little skittish.

One thing Elmer Chase knew was horses. He knew that horses usually acted jumpy or nervous around someone they didn't know. So that led Elmer to the conclusion that this man he'd met on the way to Rattlesnake was either the owner of five new horses, or he was a horse thief. And Elmer was not going to find out the hard way—by asking.

The stranger grinned—was it Elmer's overactive imagination or was this man's grin cruel as well?—and said, "Well, I'm not going to town, so you'll have to ride on alone." As he turned to go, much to Elmer's relief, he added, "And I'd turn you down even if I was going to Rattlesnake. I don't like company, especially strangers."

He patted his gun for emphasis and moved on.

If I was standing on my own two feet right now, Elmer thought, my legs would be as steady as two young saplings in a thunderstorm.

Elmer Chase thanked his stars all the way to town. This was one story he wasn't anxious to tell—not in Rattlesnake, at least. Maybe tomorrow when he was back in Wolf Creek, he'd sit down with old Prent and a bottle of whiskey by the fireside some evening and swap stories.

CHAPTER 17

IN her whole life, Mattie Quinn had never dreamed that she'd one day end up in a damp, cramped jail cell. Waking up on that hard cot made her feel ten years older. When she looked out of the rusty iron bars of her jailhouse window on the first morning, all she saw was fog. The heavy mist permeated her cell, chilling her to the bone. Mattie felt that the fog mirrored her own life at the moment.

The fog outside her cell was like a gray curtain that hid a large expanse of grass range with buttes dotting the landscape in the distance. She wished finding Joe's killer was as easy as a strong ray of sun burning off the fog.

Would she have been better off by telling Gordy Cobb the truth about visiting Amos Blackiston? If only someone had witnessed her ride off. Jefferson Birch knew the truth, but now that she was in jail, she didn't think he'd tell Cobb.

Marshal Cobb came in with a mug of coffee and handed it to her. Before he left, he asked "Is there anything else you need, Mrs. Quinn? Just let me know." He paused and added, "This is the first time I've ever jailed a woman."

"Oh really? It wasn't noticeable," she said drily. Mattie sighed and turned back to the window. A weak ray of sunshine broke through the bars. The morning fog was finally burning off.

Yesterday in the late afternoon, Marshal Cobb had gone with one of the Collins boys. She'd heard the boy, the one named Nathan, burst into Cobb's office and tell the marshal, in between gasps to catch his breath, that five of their horses were gone. Gimpy Higgins was brought in to look after her while the marshal went out to the Collins ranch to investigate.

Gimpy worked various odd jobs around town. Some said he wasn't much of a talker because he was old and getting deaf and others said it was because he'd spent so much of his time living as a hermit during the years he panned gold in eastern Montana Territory.

But Gordy Cobb was back on the job this morning. After eating a plate of greasy eggs, limp bacon, and dry, hard biscuits from the saloon, Mattie wasn't sure she was ready to find out what else was in store for her today. It was enough to find out last night that the townsfolk weren't breaking down the door to string her up.

Mattie heard someone walk in the door of the jailhouse.

The marshal spoke first. "I was wondering when I'd see you here."

"I heard the Collinses had a little trouble out on their ranch yesterday." The sound of Birch's voice was somehow very comforting to Mattie.

"So they did. Five of their horses were stolen. They're a small outfit, so it hit them pretty hard."

Another familiar voice said, "Well, don't you think you should release Mrs. Quinn, Marshal? She's obviously not the desperado you think she is."

"Now hold on a minute, Omaha."

That was just like Omaha—he's so impetuous, Mattie thought.

The marshal continued, "I'd like to let her go, but the evidence that she rustled those Blackiston horses is still too strong right now for me to just let her walk away."

Omaha raised his voice. "Damn it, Gordy. You know as well as I do that Mattie just lost her husband and has been trying to keep the ranch together, not to mention trying to discover who's behind all the trouble at the ranch. When did the woman have time to steal horses?"

"If it were just up to me, I'd let her out in a minute. But you know what the townsfolk might think. And you know Mattie Quinn had a motive to steal Blackiston's horses."

Before Omaha could rant some more, Birch said in a reasonable voice, "But the only horses found by Grundy were Capwell's."

The marshal answered, "I know. That's why I've given Grundy permission to search the rest of the Quinn land."

"What?" Omaha shouted.

Someone in the office started pacing agitatedly.

Birch said, "Grundy's within his rights to search, but Marshal, I think the law should be along for the ride."

Cobb sighed heavily. "Birch, you know I got other things to do. I know what you're thinking—Grundy could just wander into town with the rest of the stolen horses and claim they were on Mattie Quinn's land. But I can't help you there. If you're so concerned, you should go find Grundy and stay with him."

Omaha said, "If Blackiston's horses are found on her property, would that give the marshal here cause to charge her with the murder of Amos Blackiston? And why haven't I been arrested? If she was the leader of these rustlers, wouldn't I most likely be one of the gang?"

The marshal spoke up. "I haven't found a connection between the rustling and Blackiston's murder, so I probably wouldn't charge her with the killing unless someone came forward with information that she'd been seen at his ranch." Cobb paused, then added, "Besides, Birch here swears that he was with Mrs. Quinn until she started to fix supper. Isn't that right, Birch?"

It was a short silence in which Mattie could hear her heart pounding.

Fortunately, Omaha again asked the marshal why he hadn't arrested all the Quinn ranch hands.

"Because even though Chester Grundy brought the Capwell horses back to show me, I just can't believe that there's any truth to it. But if he brings back the Blackiston horses, I may have to arrest all of you."

Omaha exploded, "Birch, get back to the ranch and find Grundy before he . . . "

"Can't do that, Omaha," Birch said. "I've got something else to do today."

Mattie's heart sank to the pit of her stomach. Who was going to stick up for her, if not Birch?

Omaha growled, "I thought you were paid to protect Mrs. Quinn's interests."

"That's what I'm doing," Birch replied calmly.

"Then I'd better go back," Omaha said. "As soon as I see Mattie. I mean, Mrs. Quinn."

Birch told the marshal, "I'd like to see Mrs. Quinn first for a few minutes, if that's all right."

"Sure. Birch, leave your gun on the desk and I'll take you both back."

"No, I need to talk to her alone," Birch said. "I'll make it short."

Omaha protested, "Now wait a minute, Birch . . . "

There was a scuffling sound and keys jangling. Then the marshal saying, "You stay out here, Omaha. Only one visitor at a time."

Omaha started to argue, but Birch murmured something that shut him up.

For Mattie, it was a relief to finally see Birch. He wore a wrinkled black suit, white shirt that was frayed at the cuffs, string tie, and a black hat. She wondered if he wore the outfit because it was Sunday or if he'd just run out of denims. She noted that he also wore his gunbelt, although it was empty at the moment. At least Birch wasn't taking Sunday off for religious observance. Mattie had a feeling that she didn't have enough time left, even here under the marshal's "protection," for the investigator she'd hired to trot off to church. It was hard to feel optimistic when you just spent the night in jail.

"How's the marshal treating you?" Birch asked.

"Oh, like a queen," she replied, holding up her extra

blanket. "But I have a complaint about the food. I think Cobb has a deal with Bo, the saloon owner."

Birch grimaced and nodded. "I ate there a few nights ago, the night the old man was killed in the alley. The food still hasn't settled."

Mattie wanted to laugh, but her heart wasn't in it. She managed a half-hearted smile and nodded.

"So, do you have any more bad news for me, Mr. Birch?"

Reluctantly, Birch shook his head. "I'm afraid I haven't found out anything that would clear you yet."

Mattie crossed her arms and muttered, "Next thing you know, the marshal will be charging me with my own husband's murder and burning down my own barn." After a minute of silence, she turned back to Birch. "So why did you come down here?"

"I wanted to make sure you were being treated right and that the locals weren't inviting you to be guest of honor at a little necktie party."

That's all you came here for? she wanted to scream. Instead, Mattie gestured with her arms, indicating her small cell. "As you can see, I am doing fine. Apparently the townsfolk weren't drunk enough last night to storm the jail."

Birch frowned and said, "Don't you think it's odd that only Capwell's horses were found in your pasture? Why not Blackiston's?"

Mattie sighed. If she'd had more room, she would have paced her cell. It seemed that they just kept going around in circles and not getting anywhere. When would Birch find out something useful, something that would let her go home to her ranch, to the place she had built with Joe?

Mattie remembered the marshal being called away yesterday afternoon. "Did you know about the horses taken from the Collins place?"

Birch asked sharply, "When did it happen?"

She told him just as Marshal Cobb poked his head in and

called, "Time's up, Birch. Omaha wants to see Mrs. Quinn as well."

"Birch reached out and squeezed Mattie's hand. "Don't worry. I'll get you out of this or die trying."

Mattie believed him, but there was little comfort in the alternative.

CHAPTER 18

WHILE Omaha visited with Mattie Quinn, Birch holstered his gun and took a turn around the office, studying a few new wanted posters scattered around the walls.

Marshal Cobb spoke first. "There was another murder here in Rattlesnake a few days ago. You know anything about it?"

Birch froze, then said, "Tell me about it."

Cobb sat at his desk and crossed his arms. "Seems there was this old fellow, Stinky. He worked at the stables whenever he needed money to buy whiskey, which was just about every day. Stinky was seen in Bo's saloon not long before he was killed. His throat was cut and he was left in an alley near Bo's."

Birch waited.

Cobb went on. "Bo identified you as one of the two customers there when Stinky left."

Birch said, "Stinky didn't leave. He was kicked out."

Cobb raised his eyebrows. "How's that?"

"He was kicked out by Chester Grundy. I don't suppose Bo told you that."

"Go on."

"No, I didn't think he would. I bet Chester Grundy has a way of making people forget he was there." Birch leaned up against some of the posters. "After Grundy yelled at the old man and kicked him out, he told me it was in my best interests to leave town and forget about Mattie Quinn."

Cobb rubbed his chin and stared off into space. "I guess I should have figured it. I always thought Chester Grundy was

116

nothing but a troublemaker. I'll have to have another talk with Bo."

After a few minutes of silence, Birch turned to the marshal and demanded, "What about the stolen Collins horses? Have you found the rustlers yet?"

"No, I haven't found the damned thieves yet, Birch," the marshal replied irritably. "I'm investigating the murder right now, so if you'd like to take up the search, well, be my guest."

"Did you find anything that might tell you which way the rustlers might have taken the horses? Five horses couldn't have just disappeared."

Cobb had started to go through a stack of wanted posters to weed out the old ones. He put his work aside and gave Birch his full attention.

"You know, I've been working as a lawman for almost ten years now. Don't you think I ought to know my job by now?" He stood up and paced, then said hesitantly, "There were no signs to read. The ground was already pretty well trampled by cattle and the horses ridden by the Collinses." Cobb shook his head and added, "I wish I could say that I found a dozen witnesses who saw the rustlers and could identify every blamed one of them, but I'm afraid that's not the case here. Again." He picked up the posters and sent them flying across the room.

Birch watched Cobb for a moment, then started to pick up the posters from the office floor. The lawman stood there and watched, apparently gathering his composure by running a hand over his face.

Birch put the stack of wanted bills back on Cobb's desk and said, "You know, I don't envy your job. It can't be easy trying to walk the line between the powerful men in this town and what's right." He started for the door.

"Omaha's still in there with Mrs. Quinn," Cobb reminded him. "Aren't you going to wait?"

Birch paused and said, "No. He can find his way back to the ranch without my help."

"What are you going to do next, Birch?"

The former Texas Ranger shrugged and left.

Birch wasn't sure what he was going to do after leaving the marshal's office. He'd been meaning to go have a talk with Luther Capwell for some time, but something always got in the way.

During the few days that Birch had spent on Mattie Quinn's ranch, he'd found out that Capwell's spread was on the other side of Rattlesnake. The property bordered another offshoot of the Powder River. All Birch had to do was ride on out there.

Then it came to him—a moment of true inspiration. Where would he find all the sinners socializing on a Sunday morning?

He walked over to the most likely place for worship to be held in such a small town—Bo's saloon. It was empty except for Bo.

Was it his imagination or did Bo look slightly uncomfortable when he walked through the door?

"I thought this would be where the town would worship on Sunday morning," Birch said.

Bo shook his head and said, "Not in Rattlesnake. The town wives wouldn't stand for it. Go to the general store."

Birch nodded a thank you and left.

The store was crowded when he got there. Birch noticed that the crowd consisted mostly of women and families and the service was almost over. The fire and brimstone lasted fifteen more minutes, then everyone got up to stretch and greet each other. They carried the murmur of conversation out onto the street. Birch was just about to ask someone to point out the Collins family when he overheard part of a conversation.

"That's terrible, Kate. How will you cope without the horses?" The speaker, a raw-boned woman about fifty, addressed a slender blond woman in her midthirties.

Kate shook her head. "I don't know, Adelaide. Maybe we could hook up with another small outfit for the drive."

Adelaide clucked her tongue. "Such a shame. I wish we could help, but we just don't have the horses or men. You know that Quinn woman is in jail. They think she was the head of a rustling ring."

A stocky dark-haired man approached the two women. "We ought to get back to the ranch, Kate."

She looked around. "Where are the boys?"

The other woman had drifted off, leaving the Collinses alone. Birch walked up to them.

"Mr. and Mrs. Collins?" He took his hat off and continued. "My name is Jefferson Birch. I'd like to talk to you about your stolen horses, if you don't mind."

The husband and wife looked at each other. Kate finally said, "I'll go look for the boys while you two talk."

When she was gone, Collins formally introduced himself. "Matthew Collins. What can I do for you, Mr. Birch?"

Birch explained who he worked for and what he wanted. When he was finished, Collins nodded.

"Fact is, most of us small ranchers don't think Mattie Quinn is a rustler. I'll be happy to oblige. Follow me."

They walked over to a horse and buggy and two saddled horses.

"The boys ride the horses on Sunday and I ride with Katie in the buggy." Matthew Collins walked over to one of the horses, grabbed his head, and pulled it down. "Here's the earmark. Think you can remember it? We don't brand 'em. I think this is less painful."

The earmark was two deep parallel cuts on the left ear. Birch nodded. "I can remember. What do the cow ponies look like?"

Collins screwed his face up in thought and recited, "Two spotted, two brown, and one black with white on the throat and forehead. One of the brown has a light-colored mane."

"Thanks." Birch put his hat back on and shook Collins's hand.

"Hope you get the son-of-a-bitch that done this."

Birch gave a short nod and said, "So do I."

As he was leaving, Birch noticed Luther Capwell strolling toward him.

"So we meet again, Birch," he greeted heartily as he sized up the lanky ex-Ranger.

"Your hired gun came out to the Quinn place and found your stolen horses," Birch informed the cattle baron. "Mattie Quinn is locked up right now, but I'm sure it won't be for long."

Capwell beamed with confidence as he replied, "I hope you can find the proof you need. But I've heard rumors around here that you're asking questions about me."

"You're on my list," Birch said shortly. He didn't feel the need to add that the list was extremely short.

Capwell laughed. "If I were a rustler, why would I take my own horses?"

Birch studied the man quietly. "Your horses were the only ones found on the Quinn property. And I assume they were returned to you?"

"Of course. What else would Gordy Cobb do with 'em?" Capwell chuckled. "And the horses are none the worse for wear. Those rustlers took real good care of 'em. But then, Mattie was always good with horses."

"Why, you bastard!" Omaha pushed Birch aside and threw himself at Capwell, shouting, "She didn't do it and you know it!"

The two men rolled around on the ground, Omaha trying to get punches in and Capwell throwing an arm up to protect his face. Birch dove in and grabbed the Quinn ranch hand. Birch noted that Capwell, while he didn't fight back physically, had reached into his brocade vest for a derringer. The former Texas Ranger pulled an unarmed Omaha off just in time.

Omaha turned on Birch. "Are you crazy? Whose side are you on anyway? You should have let me alone with him."

With that, Omaha turned and spat on Luther Capwell.

Birch noted that the Sunday worshippers were gathered on the edge of the scene. Capwell finished brushing some of the dust off and stuck his hand out to Birch, saying, "I should thank you."

"No, you shouldn't," Birch said with disdain. "I saw you reaching for that pocket cannon and I wasn't about to let Omaha take a lead ball in the gut."

He scanned the crowd, then walked away from Luther Capwell.

CHAPTER 19

BIRCH needed a drink. He stopped at the still empty saloon and tossed down a whiskey before another customer entered. Since it was Sunday, a saloon shouldn't expect business to pick up before late afternoon. But atheists and travelers walked into saloons at all hours. This man looked like both, but Birch wasn't sure whether the man was from this area or not—not until the man took off his fur hat. There wasn't much in the way of fur down in the southern Montana Territory. Birch made an educated guess that this man was from up north where fur trading was common.

The stranger laid his saddlebags on a table and bellied up to the bar. "Bottle of red-eye," he said in a deep, rough voice. Spinning a silver coin on top of the well-polished surface, he added, "And a glass."

Birch noted that the man was in his fifties, at least, with white hair that clung to his head where the hat had sat and a small bald spot near the back. Like most cowboys and fur traders, his face was weathered and lined like a Lewis and Clark map.

When his bottle arrived, he poured himself a generous helping, then turned to Birch. "Can I pour you one, too, friend? You either been eyeing me or this bottle for the last few minutes."

"Sure. Thanks." Birch sipped his red-eye and observed, "You look like you're going somewhere."

The man laughed, quite a different laugh from Luther Capwell. "I'll say. I'm going home. Been in town just one night and I'm ready to go back now."

Birch nodded and introduced himself. They sat down at a table.

The friendly stranger bobbed his head and replied, "Elmer Chase is the name. I'm from a little place up north called Wolf Creek." The man looked around and added, "This is a big place compared to Wolf Creek. Yes sir."

Birch smiled. He liked Elmer. "Are you a trader?"

"Yep," Elmer said as he poured himself another. He looked over at Birch's empty glass and filled it, too. "How'd you know?"

Birch pointed to the hat. Elmer laughed again.

"What are you doing here in town?"

Elmer grunted and said, "Thought I'd pick up some snake wire. I have a few critters up there on my land and they keep knocking down my split-rail fence."

Birch was enjoying talking to Elmer Chase. This wasn't someone whom he suspected of murder or rustling or anything. And he was generous with his whiskey. But if Elmer Chase had come down from up north, there was a slight chance he'd passed the Capwell ranch on his way here. Maybe at the same time the Collins' horses were stolen. It was a long shot.

"So you've only been here overnight, right?" Birch asked.

"Yep. Wolf Creek's far enough away for an overnight stay. And I'm getting too old to bed down out on the range at night."

"I still camp out when I'm traveling, but every year the ground seems to get harder," Birch said.

Elmer chuckled. "Well, if you get hired on with the big outfits around here, I bet you won't spend too many cold, lonely nights on the range."

So this fur trader had taken Birch for a ranch hand. He decided to go along.

"I guess since you're only here for a short time, you don't know what's been happening around here," Birch replied.

"No. What do you mean?" Elmer leaned across the table

and listened as Birch told him about Blackiston's murder and the stolen horses. He finished up with a lurid account of Mattie Quinn's subsequent arrest, which left the old man shaking his head.

"Terrible thing about that woman," Elmer commiserated. "Nope. I don't believe a recent widow would have the heart to go out and rustle up horses. Now if anyone was a rustler, it was that mean-looking fellow I met on the trip in here."

Birch leaned forward. "A mean-looking fellow?"

"Well, it's a mighty long trip here to Rattlesnake from Wolf Creek. Takes almost the whole day and no one to talk to but the sorry-looking cayuse I'm riding." Elmer settled into his story. Birch could tell that the man from Wolf Creek had had practice. "So when I run across this stranger riding along with a string of five horses, I call out real friendly, asking him if he's headed toward Rattlesnake."

Elmer freshened his whiskey and continued. "This fellow's got evil eyes, the kind of guy who'd rather kill you than have a drink with you. Since I got a closer look at him, I'm sorry I ever opened my mouth. And he gets real mean, telling me to mind my own business. Well, I wasn't born yesterday. I know when to keep my thoughts to myself and I let him go on."

When Elmer Chase was finished with his story, Birch was smiling. "Was he headed into town like you asked him?"

"No, he was headed out the opposite way that I was going. But I couldn't tell which way he was headed when I first met him because he was just coming onto the road, like he'd taken those horses to the river for a drink."

"What time of day did you meet him?"

Elmer rubbed his chin and looked up. "Oh, I'd say middle of the afternoon, maybe early afternoon. Can't say exactly because I don't carry one of those pocket watches."

Birch felt like he was finally getting somewhere on this case. On top of a third shot, he had just listened to a description of Chester Grundy leading the five horses away from the Collins ranch. He clapped Elmer on the arm and thanked him.

"If you're ever up near Wolf Creek," Elmer said in parting, "drop in. I bet you got lots of interesting stories to tell. Me and my friend, Prent, just love to sit around the fireplace and swap stories."

Birch doubted he'd ever get up there with winter so close by, but he promised to make the effort.

Mounting Cactus and riding out of town, Birch felt determined to get to the bottom of it all. Mattie Quinn would be safe enough in jail for the moment—most of the town didn't think she'd done it—but you can never tell. It only took one man to start filling people's heads with all sorts of ideas that weren't true. Pretty soon, you had a lynch mob on your hands.

Birch recalled the time he lost a man who was accused of robbing a bank. No one had been able to definitely identify him, but some of the witnesses said that he looked the most like the bank robber they'd seen (and they'd only seen part of his face because he wore a bandanna over his nose and mouth).

So Birch was the Ranger assigned to take him to jail to await trial. It was Saturday evening in Alvarez, and as they rode down the street toward the jail men came out of the saloons and followed. Silently.

Birch knew that something was wrong. The accused man looked uneasy and pleaded with Birch to break into a gallop.

"I have a wife and three children," the man begged. "I didn't rob the bank, but I want to live long enough for my neighbor to come into town and tell the law here that I was helping him mend fences at the time of the robbery."

But it was too late to break into a gallop. Two big men stepped out in front of Birch and the accused man. They took the reins. Two more men trained shotguns on them and ordered them down from their horses.

"Stop this at once," Birch ordered. "This man has not been sentenced. He's innocent until proven guilty."

One of the men, apparently the leader, replied, "Not in our court. We lost a lot of money from that robbery. There are people who had saved for years to make their lives easier and this man has taken it all away."

Birch pointed out, "We haven't found the money in his possession. Wait until then."

"We think he's guilty," the leader said, indicating the mob. "That's enough." He ordered someone to get a rope.

Birch reached for his Colt and a shotgun was shoved in his gut. Another man took his gun and two more men held his arms while he struggled to save the accused man.

They led the accused man to a tree on the edge of Alvarez. Birch averted his eyes when the man was hanged. He died still protesting his innocence.

Later, they found the man who'd robbed the bank in a nearby town, gambling his loot away. Town officials got suspicious of where the money had come from and held the real bank robber for questioning and soon found out that he was wanted in two other territories for bank robberies.

People in Alvarez walked around looking sheepish for days. They rallied enough to bring food and money to the widow and the children. No one was ever charged with killing an innocent man, although Birch tried his damnedest to arrest someone.

Birch ran into Marshal Cobb on the way out of town.

"So you met Luther Capwell," Cobb remarked.

"I sure did," Birch replied. "And I'm convinced that he's behind the rustling."

"But his horses were stolen just like Blackiston's and Collins's," the marshal pointed out. "Why would he rustle his own horses?"

Birch shrugged and said, "He got them back, didn't he? And we never found the other stolen horses."

"Chester Grundy is looking into that right now."

Birch added, "On Mattie Quinn's property. But I wonder if Grundy is really looking."

The lawman furrowed his brow. "What are you going to do, Birch?"

"I'm going back to the ranch to look for Grundy." Birch spurred Cactus on.

When Birch got back to the Quinn ranch, it was quiet. Charley was staying around the main house to keep an eye on it.

"Where's Omaha and Slim?" Birch asked.

Charley pointed toward the south part of the land, and said, "Omaha came back about an hour ago and went off that way. Said something about looking for Grundy."

"And Slim went with him?"

The ranch hand shook his head. "Haven't seen Slim today. Last night he told me he was going in to hear the preacher this morning."

Birch frowned, trying to remember seeing Slim in the crowd. There had been so many people there that he really couldn't say. Well, it was no matter, he thought. Mattie Quinn was more important.

"Which way did Grundy head?"

Charley thought a moment, then pointed to the south. "He said he was going to check over there. Said Mrs. Quinn could hide horses up in that rocky area. Omaha went after him about an hour ago. Said he wanted to make sure Grundy wasn't going to bring those horses on our property, then claim we stole 'em."

Birch nodded and thanked Charley. "If Slim or Omaha come back, ask them to stick around. I'll be back soon. We have to figure out what to do next."

"Birch?"

"Yeah?"

Charley rubbed the back of his neck and asked, "You think you'll be able to get Mrs. Quinn out of jail soon?"

The former Texas Ranger tipped his hat to the worried ranch hand and said, "I'll make sure she's out before the cattle drive."

"If she's going to run her ranch right," Charley said, indicating his begrudging respect for the widow, "then she's going to have to know what it's like to drive the cattle to market."

"Sure enough, Charley," Birch said, spurring Cactus on south.

CHAPTER 20

JOHN "Omaha" Johanson was eye-popping mad after Birch pulled him off Luther Capwell. Omaha was convinced Capwell was responsible for Joe's death and the terrible things that had happened on Mattie's ranch since. He hadn't been able to help himself when he rushed at Luther Capwell, ready to knock his head off. Until Birch, that traitor, had pulled him off Capwell. Omaha had wondered if Birch was making a better deal for himself. Maybe Capwell offered Birch more money to forget Mattie Quinn. Maybe the great detective was working for Capwell now.

Omaha gritted his teeth and rode out to the ranch, fuming over Birch's lack of concern for Mattie.

Although he'd never admit it to anyone, Omaha had a soft spot for Mattie Quinn, even when Joe was alive. Of course, he never let it show, especially around Joe, but now he had thoughts about asking her to be his wife when the time was right—maybe a year from now. He didn't know what Charley or Slim's reasons were for staying on at a small ranch that hardly paid anything, but what kept Omaha there was Mattie Quinn.

The day had grown colder and Omaha was glad he'd worn his buckskin jacket. He planned to stop back at the bunkhouse for his guns before going off in search of Chester Grundy, even though every minute counted. Why by now, Grundy could have already snuck those rustled horses onto Mattie's land and pretended to find them.

Omaha had always had a bad feeling about Chester Grundy. He'd tried not to let those small eyes and that sneer influence him, but one day, he came across Grundy shooting small animals just for practice.

When Omaha asked him why he didn't set up tin cans for targets like most other people, Grundy replied, "They don't move like squirrels and chipmunks." Now, Omaha didn't have a real soft spot for small animals or anything, but he couldn't see the sense in killing anything alive unless a man had to fill his belly. Besides, he caught the gleam of pleasure in Grundy's face whenever he'd shot one of those helpless moving targets. After that day, Omaha had no problem disliking Chester Grundy.

As he neared the Quinn land, Omaha spied Charley out in the clearing. He had obviously been chopping wood, but was looking off in the distance with the axe by his side.

Omaha called to the ranch foreman, "Charley! Has Grundy been here for a visit yet?"

Charley hailed Omaha with his axe and yelled, "About fifteen minutes ago. Down on the back forty."

Waving his thanks, Omaha headed south without bothering to stop for his guns. There was a large outcrop of rock down that way that would be a handy place to hide horses. There had been many times in the winter that Omaha, Charley, and former ranch hands had used that rock formation for shelter when bringing back stray cattle. Slim hadn't spent a winter here on the Quinn ranch yet, but Omaha remembered showing him where it was this summer. Not many people knew about it, even those who had lived around Rattlesnake for a long time. Omaha wondered if Grundy had just headed that way by chance, or if this was a specific destination.

Leaving the shelter of trees that surrounded the Quinn main house and immediate property, the wind cut through his buckskin. He pushed his hat firmly on his head so there was no chance of it flying away, hunched down over his horse, and headed into the wind.

A short time later, Omaha spotted the high outcrop

through watery eyes, but he saw no movement. Dismounting from his horse, Omaha started to call out Grundy's name, then thought better of it. There was something eerie and forbidding about the wind whistling through the rock formation. He tied his horse to a bush that sprouted from a crack in a giant granite boulder and started to climb around until he reached a fissure in the rock, large enough for desperate ranch hands to squeeze through with winter-starved cattle. Slim stood in the shelter with about fifteen horses.

"Slim," Omaha hailed as he entered the sheltered gorge. The young cowboy started and looked up in surprise, his hand going for the gun he wore at his side. Once again, Omaha wished he'd stopped long enough at the bunkhouse to strap on his gunbelt. But it didn't seem to matter because Slim had found the rustled horses; both Collins's and Blackiston's horses were there.

Slim's face relaxed. "You startled me."

Omaha walked around the horses and inspected the brands to make sure they were all there. "So you found them."

"Uh, yeah. I remembered that you'd showed me this place a few months ago and thought I'd have a look around."

Omaha frowned as he remembered Charley telling him that Grundy had a fifteen-minute start and was definitely headed this way. Well then, how did both Quinn ranch hands get here before the Association detective?

Omaha shook his head. It was more important to protect Mattie at all costs, he thought. They had to get rid of the horses.

He said to Slim, "Grundy's around here somewhere. We'd better avoid him and get these critters off the property . . . "

Someone was coming. Omaha turned around. A hard-faced Grundy stood at the entrance.

"So you found the horses, did you?" Grundy sneered. His eyes traveled down to where Omaha's gun would normally be. "I guess you're out of luck, cowboy. I can't let you go now."

Omaha shouted, "Slim, get your gun out."

But Grundy already had his gun in his hand. The only chance they had was if Omaha bought Slim enough time to draw his gun. He saw Grundy pulling the trigger and stepped in front of the younger ranch hand. Omaha fell back from the impact of the bullet.

Omaha reached up and felt his left shoulder. It was wet, as he expected. He looked around at both Grundy and Slim facing each other, guns drawn, but his vision was getting blurry. Was it his imagination, or did everything seem to be going in slow motion? He was still waiting for a second shot when he sank into the welcoming darkness of unconsciousness.

CHAPTER 21

WHEN Birch arrived at the main house, Charley was stacking freshly cut wood. The old foreman almost dropped a bundle when the former Ranger rode up.

"You scared me half to death." Charley indicated the shotgun resting against the woodpile. "I might have shot you and asked who you were afterwards."

Birch smiled grimly and said, "Has Chester Grundy been here yet?"

Charley pointed toward the south. "He came by here less than an hour ago and headed that way. There's a small canyon out there. In the winter, when it's bitter cold, we use it for shelter when we go after a stray cow."

Birch thanked Charley and pointed Cactus in that direction when Charley added, "You're the second person who's asked that. Omaha went that way about fifteen minutes after Grundy. I thought I heard a shot a while ago, but it was so faint, I couldn't swear to it."

Birch tried to recall if Omaha had been wearing a gun on their way to town. "Charley, did Omaha stop by here and get his gun?"

The foreman thought about it for a moment and finally said, "I can't say for sure, but I don't think so."

Birch spurred Cactus into a gallop. The trail wound around through small pine wooded areas, climbing gradually. Birch had to slow Cactus down at times when the ground became treacherous, but he eventually came to an open area. Beyond the grass range, he saw the outcrop. The wind had grown colder and he wished he'd been able to stop at the bunkhouse for his warmer coat. He wore only a thin cotton shirt and his black Sunday suit jacket and the cold had reached his bones by this time.

When he had crossed the range and was closer to the gorge, he came across a gray horse. It looked like the one on which Omaha had ridden into town this morning. Birch rode up and left Cactus with Omaha's horse. Although he could have ridden his horse into the gorge, it would be better to enter on foot. There would be less chance of a surprise ambush.

Stepping cautiously through the narrow entrance, Birch drew his Navy Colt and cocked it. He could see that it was a good shelter for a cold cowboy and a few stray animals in a blizzard. As he surveyed the seemingly empty canyon, he heard a moan. With the wind whistling around the rock formation, it was hard to pinpoint but Birch knew it had to be Omaha.

He called the ranch hand's name and followed a weak voice answering "Over here." Wedged between two small boulders, Omaha was clutching a bullet-shattered shoulder. Birch sat him up and peeled his blood-caked buckskin jacket off of his left side and, working with his Bowie knife, ripped Omaha's shirt sleeve off.

Through chattering teeth, the ranch hand talked about what happened as Birch dressed the wound as best as he could. "Find Slim. He's got to be somewhere around here, too. If the horses are gone, Grundy must have shot Slim as well. I passed out before I heard the shot, though."

Birch looked around from his crouched position. "I didn't see Slim's horse when I got here."

"Maybe Grundy took Slim with him to mind that string of horses. He'll probably kill him later." Birch helped Omaha up to a sitting position and the injured man turned pasty white with the effort.

"You stay here and I'll go get Charley," Birch said.

"No." Omaha said it quietly, but there was force behind it. "Just help me to my horse and I'll ride out to get help."

With Omaha's good arm around his shoulders and Birch's arm supporting most of Omaha's weight, they made their way slowly out of the canyon. Omaha winced once when Birch helped him up on his horse.

"Go after Grundy," Omaha grimaced as he struggled to get up. His face set in grim determination to make it back to the ranch. Clinging to his horse and clutching the reins for dear life, Omaha cautioned Birch, "Be careful. Chester Grundy is as dangerous as a rattler on the end of a forked stick."

Birch patted his gunbelt soberly. "I have everything I need. You just get yourself back to the ranch and send Charley to town to warn the marshal about Grundy."

With that, he nodded to the injured man and left for Capwell's ranch.

Birch took the road that didn't go through town. He wasn't sure how many minions Capwell had in Rattlesnake and how much they might know.

Birch was pretty sure that both Grundy and Capwell weren't going to take those stolen horses to Marshal Cobb. Why should Luther Capwell return the ten horses to Blackiston's widow? She was probably going to sell the ranch to him anyway.

And Matthew Collins was of no consequence because he was a small rancher. Losing five good horses would force him to sell and move his family away from this area. Then Capwell could add the Collins land to his already fast-growing cattle empire.

It was dark by the time he reached the Capwell ranch. The main house was as large as Blackiston's place and had imported glass panes for windows, but it was obvious that there was no woman's touch here.

Horses moved restlessly in a small corral to Birch's left. Sensing a guard somewhere out in the approaching darkness, he stopped and waited.

A shadowy figure in the darkness moved in front of the

corral, probably headed for the bunkhouse. When he was gone, Birch slid down from the saddle unseen. He slapped Cactus's hindquarters, sending his horse off the Capwell property.

Crouching behind the corral, Birch slipped between the split-rail fencing and checked the horses for the Collins earmark. Five of them matched, although it was hard to tell the black from the brown in the dark.

The other ten horses that Birch counted had different earmarks that matched each other. While he'd never checked the Blackiston earmark, there was a good chance that these ten well-fed horses were the rustled string.

Birch wasn't sure what to do next. The smart thing to do would be to ride out on the road and wait for the marshal to show up, although Birch knew that Cobb would be reluctant to arrest Luther Capwell.

But there was still the matter of Slim. Where could he be? It was likely that Grundy had already killed the young cowhand, but if there was a chance Birch could get to Slim without being seen, he'd have to take it.

Leaving the corral through the far side of the fence, Birch crouched behind the feed box that sat next to the horses. A guard was lighting a hand-rolled cigarette, and from the brief flare of the match Birch saw that he was leaning against a tree—not a good thing to do when standing guard. Birch drew his gun and held it by the barrel. He didn't want to shoot the man and draw attention, he just wanted to get past the guard and buy some time. Reaching out, Birch picked up a small rock and flung it across the corral where it landed with a thunk.

The Capwell ranch hand started and brought his shotgun up, asking, "Who's there?"

As fast as he could run in a crouching position, Birch headed for the guard and brought the butt of his Colt down hard, knocking the man out. He picked up the shotgun, emptied it of its cartridges, then tossed it into the corral.

Moving carefully across the clearing, his gun at the ready, Birch headed for the side of the house. Most of the house was dark, but Birch was drawn to the light spilling out from a pair of French doors a few yards away. He slid against the wall until his shoulder was against the door frame.

From his short glances, he could see that the room was some kind of office and Luther Capwell was talking to Chester Grundy. Although the doors were made mostly of glass, Birch still couldn't hear their conversation. But he watched as Luther Capwell took a large sum of money from his desk and handed it over to Grundy.

He had to find out what they were talking about and that meant that he'd have to get inside the house. Watching the front of the building for a few minutes, Birch finally determined that it was clear and headed for the front door. It wasn't locked for the night yet and he was able to slip in easily. No one was loitering inside, so Birch headed quietly down the hall, stopping at a partially open door. He could hear their voices clearly.

"With Amos dead, you should have no problem with the widow Quinn." The voice was cold and gravelly, like Chester Grundy's voice that day they fought.

"Putting my horses on her property was a good idea," Capwell chuckled, then his voice was thoughtful as he added, "But I wish you hadn't killed that ranch hand of hers."

Grundy grunted and replied, "He would have hanged with the Quinn woman eventually. I just saved the circuit judge the trouble. The same goes for the other hands. The finger will be pointing right at them when the judge asks how Mattie Quinn did all that rustling herself."

Birch heard one of the men moving around inside the office. Capwell spoke next.

"I have to admit that I had some reservations about this whole plan from the beginning. When you came to me with what Amos had been planning and carrying out, I wasn't happy about the number of people we had to remove from our path." The speaker paused, then continued. "But it's worked out for the best. Now, what about that detective fellow, what was his name?"

"Birch," Grundy supplied. "Jefferson Birch. He's trouble. If he continues to ask questions, I can arrange to take care of him so no one will ever hear from him again. It won't look like he's been killed, not even by accident—he'll just disappear."

The barrel of a gun jammed into Birch's back and the man behind the gun said loud enough for the men in the office to hear, "Looks like you won't have to wait long, Chester."

Birch recognized the voice as belonging to Slim. Propelled by the weapon trained on him, Birch stepped into the office. Slim relieved him of his gun and tossed it to Grundy.

Luther Capwell stood there with a brandy in his hand and an amused look on his face. "Hasn't anyone told you that trespassing is bad manners, Birch?" Capwell finished his brandy and crossed the room to pour another. "Tell me, Birch. You're a reasonable man, aren't you?"

Birch replied mildly, "Reasonable enough."

"Let us say that I offered you a sum of money to get on your horse and ride out of here. Out of the county. Out of the territory." With the brandy in his hand, Capwell turned to face the former Texas Ranger and added, "Would you take it?"

"Let us say, no," Birch said simply.

"That's too bad. But I had a feeling that you had a conscience." Capwell crossed in front of Birch and turned suddenly. He said, "Oh, yes. I see it now. You were caught in my house in the dark. I mistook you for a burglar." Capwell came up close to Birch's face and added, "But that's too messy. My housekeeper would spend days trying to scrub the bloodstains out of the imported carpet." The cattle baron indicated the richly colored rug beneath their feet. "It will work just as well if you're caught outside on my land."

Birch lunged at Capwell, grabbing a fistful of his shirt.

Grundy stuck his cocked gun under Birch's nose as a re-
minder of where he was. Birch let go of Capwell reluctantly.

After straightening his collar, Luther Capwell said, "Take
him outside, boys. I don't want to know what you do with
him."

CHAPTER 22

AS he was led from the study, Birch glanced back and a smiling Capwell raised his brandy.

Accompanying Birch on one side, Slim grinned. "Bet you're surprised, aren't you, Birch? You thought I was some dumb cluck of a cowhand who was working on some backwater ranch because I couldn't get a better job. That may have been true when I first started out there, but I met Mr. Capwell a few months ago and he started paying me to keep an eye and ear open around the Quinn place."

Birch replied, "And I bet you did just that."

Slim nodded and relaxed his gun barrel slightly as he recalled, "Yeah, that Mr. Capwell is real smart. I'm learning a lot from him."

Birch smiled back, confusing the traitorous cowboy. "Yeah, real smart. Why, he's so smart, he's setting you up as one of the . . ."

At this point, Grundy poked Birch's side with his gun and said gruffly, "Hey! Enough talking. Shut up."

Birch decided that Grundy wouldn't mind talking about his kills. When he was back in the study talking to Capwell, he seemed eager to boast about them. There were one or two things Birch needed to know, and if he distracted Grundy long enough he might find a way to escape.

Birch spoke up. "I got a question."

"I said shut up and I mean it," Grundy jabbed Birch's ribs again.

Birch continued, "Why would Capwell want Joe Quinn killed?"

Grundy was silent for a moment, probably trying to decide

if this was a trick. But the urge to talk about it must have finally overcome his caution and he said, "Capwell didn't order that killing. That was paid for by Amos Blackiston."

So that part was just as Birch had guessed. He tried again. "So why was Blackiston killed?"

Grundy snorted, "Because he was too impatient to wait for ranchers to be pushed off their land by the 'accidents' that Mr. Capwell arranged. Mr. Capwell called Amos Blackiston a liability, whatever that is."

Birch knew that word very well. He had just become one himself.

Grundy needed no more coaxing from Birch. He rolled on with his explanation. He must have figured that Birch was a dead man, anyway. "So Mr. Capwell made the best of a bad situation by framing Mattie Quinn for Blackiston's murder."

Birch asked, "So that's why the horses were stolen in the first place. Then why didn't it end with Capwell's horses being found on the Quinn land? Why did you rustle the Blackiston and Collins horses, too?"

Grundy was silent for a moment as if thinking that one over. Then he said, "Well, he must have just wanted to make sure that Mattie Quinn was framed good."

"But he kept the stolen horses, Grundy," Birch argued. "Doesn't that tell you something?"

After another silence, two reluctant voices, Grundy's and Slim's, asked, "What?"

Birch filled them in. "That his ranch can't be doing so well after all. He kept stolen horses. Why else would he do that? He was going to sell them on the drive in a few weeks."

Birch knew he was going out on a limb, but the only way to try to escape was to distract both of them. He already had Slim wondering what Grundy had kept Birch from saying. Now he was undermining Grundy's faith in Capwell. But the truth was that he had no idea why Capwell had stolen those horses and concealed them on his ranch.

Grundy explained, "But earlier today we brought the

horses to that gorge to make sure that Mattie Quinn was blamed. Mr. Capwell has always been fair with me."

He knows you'll kill him if he isn't, Birch thought. He was beginning to think the situation was hopeless when a suspicious sound drew Grundy's attention away.

"You watch Birch," he ordered Slim. Grundy slipped into the darkness to look for the source of the noise.

Birch half-hoped it was the marshal, but wondered if Cobb had enough sense to stay alert. He couldn't risk calling out a warning.

Slim said in a low voice, "What was it you were going to say that Grundy stopped you from saying?"

So he was interested after all. Maybe Slim wasn't as stupid as he appeared. Birch told him about the conversation he'd overheard in the study just a minute before Slim caught him.

"You're headed for a fall," Birch explained, "with the other hands, Charley and Omaha, as part of the gang. And when Capwell's through with you, no one will believe you even if you do say anything about working for Luther Capwell. He's a big man in this county and it'll be your word against his."

Slim was smiling when Birch finished. "You're just trying to outsmart me, Birch. I don't believe a word you say. Omaha's dead. I watched Grundy shoot him."

Birch smiled and said, "Omaha is very much alive. His shoulder hurts like hell, but he'll live. He's gone after the marshal. In fact, that may have been Cobb riding up."

Slim giggled nervously. "Still don't believe you. You're making this all up." They could hear Grundy approaching. In a low voice, Slim added, "I won't say anything to Grundy about what you just tried to do."

Birch laughed and said, "As a favor? Heck, go ahead and tell him."

Slim's eyes slid to the side and he licked his lips agitatedly. "No, not as a favor. I just don't think we need to tell him . . ."

Birch said loudly, "Why not? You afraid of what he might do to you?"

"Shut up!" Slim hissed.

Grundy appeared, a rope in his hand, fashioning a noose. He did it easily and expertly, as if he'd done this many times before.

"Did he give you any trouble while I was gone, Slim?"

"Uh, no, Chester. He was quiet."

Birch addressed Grundy. "I told him about your talk with Capwell. How you plan to throw him to the wolves after he's gotten Capwell what he wants."

Grundy turned to Slim and asked in a sharp voice, "And you believed him?"

"No, Chester," Slim said defensively. "No. I just figured he was trying to turn me against Mr. Capwell."

Grundy studied Slim's nervous face for a moment, seemed satisfied, and nodded. "You go get me a horse after I tie Birch's hands."

They were standing under a large cottonwood tree and Grundy looped the free end of the rope over a branch about ten feet up. He drew a smaller piece of rope out of his pocket and, with Slim training his gun on their prisoner, proceeded to tie Birch's hands behind his back.

"What was that sound earlier, Chester?" Slim asked.

"Just one of the horses acting a little wild. Go get me that horse now."

Slim left and Grundy put the noose around Birch's neck.

A yell rose from the corral, and Grundy, momentarily distracted, turned in that direction. Birch took the opportunity to kick out, connecting his boot with the back of Grundy's knee. Grundy let out a groan and knelt, his gun hand drooping slightly. Another well-placed kick sent Grundy's gun flying into the darkness and still another kick to the hired gun's gut collapsed him altogether.

Birch shrugged his head out of the noose. He wouldn't be much good standing around waiting for Grundy to recover, so he started toward the corral, running sideways like a crab to make the least possible target for some trigger-happy Capwell guard.

Two men emerged from the corral. Slim was in front, the marshal walking behind.

When Cobb spotted Birch, Cobb called out, "I wasn't sure about this one. I know he works for Mrs. Quinn, but he acted as if he were protecting Capwell's property. So I kept him within my sights."

"I never thought I'd say this, Marshal," Birch began, "but I sure am glad to see you."

They walked back to where Grundy lay groaning and Cobb clapped handcuffs on both men, then released Birch's hands.

Marshal Cobb handed Birch what was presumably Slim's gun and said, "You watch these two fellows while I round up Capwell. He's in the house?"

Birch nodded and waited. A few minutes went by before the marshal came back empty-handed. "I don't see him anywhere. I guess he's slipped past us. I'll just take these gentlemen in for now. Tomorrow, I'll send out a posse."

Birch accompanied the marshal to the corral and helped him put the prisoners on horses.

"You coming, Birch?" Marshal Cobb asked, holding the reins of his horse plus the two others in one hand and keeping his gun trained on them with his other hand.

Birch replied, "My gun is back in the house, Marshal. Do you need me or can you handle these two yourself?"

The lawman nodded solemnly. "They're not going anywhere except jail, if that's what you mean."

Glad to have an excuse to stay back, Birch said, "Then I'll just take a look around while I'm here."

"Be careful, Birch," the marshal called out over his shoulder as he led Grundy and Slim away. "Capwell's still out there somewhere."

Birch remembered that there was still a guard unaccounted for—the one he'd knocked out when he was trying to get to the house. When he returned to where he'd left the unconscious man, the ground was empty. Birch concluded that the sound that Grundy had gone to investigate was the sound of the guard taking a horse and leaving the ranch.

Back at the main house, Birch found his gun on Capwell's desk, the bullets removed. Just in case the guard or Capwell were still around, Birch loaded his Navy Colt and kept it at the ready.

He headed out behind the main house to the barn, proceeding with caution. Birch wasn't about to get caught again.

As he drew closer, he noticed the faint light of a kerosene lantern emanating from under the barn doors. Someone was preparing an escape.

Creeping along the front of the barn, Birch found a small door open along the side of the barn and he slipped in. The heady smell of horses, hay, and leather mingled together and overpowered Birch's sense of smell. He stayed out of sight behind a large stack of bales, cautiously looking out from behind the haystack toward the light. Luther Capwell was dragging an ornate leather saddle off of a saddle prop.

By his side was a brown leather satchel that Birch guessed was filled with money. Other than these items, Capwell appeared to be unarmed, but Birch was still mindful of the derringer Capwell had almost pulled out of his gold brocade vest earlier in the day.

Winded from his efforts, Capwell put the saddle down and picked up the lantern to look for a bit for the horse. Birch stepped forward and aimed his gun at the fugitive.

"Put the lantern down, Capwell, and your hands up," Birch announced. "I'm taking you in for the murder of Amos Blackiston."

Capwell looked startled for a moment, then smiled. "I don't think you want to do that, Birch. If I offer you enough money, you'll let me go." He indicated the satchel by his feet. "Take it. There's enough money in there for you to live very well."

Birch glanced briefly at the satchel, and in that second Capwell dropped the kerosene lantern. The sound of breaking glass was accompanied by the whooshing sound of hay catching fire. Then there was a wall of fire between Birch and Luther Capwell. The cattle baron grabbed his satchel and ran to the front of the barn, slipping out the door just as Birch fired a warning shot.

Birch tried to follow, but the fire had spread too quickly. It was a lucky thing for Capwell that the fire had blocked off all exits for Birch.

Birch heard frightened horses trying to kick down their stalls. Flames licked at the small wooden cubicles that were now death traps for the horses. Smoke stung his eyes and seared his lungs if he breathed too deeply. If he acted quickly, Birch thought he could probably save the horses and his own life.

Springing into action, Birch opened the stall doors, then headed for the back wall, hoping that the horses would have enough sense to follow. The flames had already engulfed the front part of the barn and were working their way toward the back fast.

On first glance, the wall appeared solid enough, but upon closer inspection, he found that the wood was rotting. He picked up a solid piece of lumber that was propped up against the wall and started hammering away at the wall until the decayed wood began to give way. When he had removed enough planks from the wall for the horses to escape, Birch staggered outside, coughing up the smoke that he'd inhaled and trying to replace it with the cold night air.

The horses that had followed him snorted several times, shook their heads, and ran off in all directions to get away from the burning barn.

Birch headed back to the corral to count the rustled horses. Sure enough, one was missing. Capwell had escaped.

Cactus was still where Birch had left him. The former Texas Ranger was grateful that he'd concealed his horse so

Capwell hadn't spotted him and taken Cactus, who was outfitted with a saddle.

Birch normally hated tracking outlaws at night. When he was a Texas Ranger, night tracking was difficult at best, and impossible at worst. But the tracks he found outside the corral gave a clear indication of which direction Luther Capwell was headed. Birch was surprised that the fugitive cattle baron would head toward Rattlesnake, but he spurred Cactus in that direction.

CHAPTER 23

LUTHER Capwell wished he'd gotten out of the barn with the saddle. He wasn't used to riding a horse bareback.

When Luther had left Birch in the burning barn, he'd had the presence of mind to take his satchel of money and a bit. Although Capwell was used to having one of his ranch hands saddle up his horse, he somehow managed to get the bit in this horse's mouth and attach the reins with a minimum of trouble.

Getting on a horse with no saddle was another problem that Capwell solved quickly. He sat on the split-rail fence and slid onto the horse's back. But the fugitive cattle king found that he had no way to attach the satchel to the horse, so he ended up clutching it. It was clumsy and uncomfortable, but it couldn't be helped.

During his escape from the barn, Luther Capwell wasn't certain where he would head, but after leaving Birch in there to burn to death, he knew what he had to do if he wanted to try to save his life here in Montana Territory. He would have to kill again.

Capwell headed toward Rattlesnake at a full gallop. The marshal would be traveling slow with his two prisoners, so Luther should be able to catch up in a few minutes. He kept his eyes fixed on the road ahead until he saw three shapes on horses.

The lead shape had unholstered his gun and was asking, "Birch, is that you?" when Capwell rode up behind Slim and drew his derringer. He only had one shot left and he would have to make it count. Just as Cobb turned around and caught sight of him, Capwell fired. The lawman tumbled off his horse and lay sprawled on the ground, a surprised look on his face. Capwell slid off his horse and searched the body for handcuff keys, then released Grundy and Slim.

"Didn't think you'd make it," Grundy said, rubbing his wrists. "What's the plan now? We should probably get out of town."

"I'm all for that," Slim piped up.

Capwell shook his head. "We still have some unfinished business in Rattlesnake."

Grundy frowned and glanced at Capwell's hand. He had taken the marshal's gun, the only gun they had, and Grundy wasn't about to argue with a man carrying a dead man's gun.

"What about Birch?" he asked.

Capwell grinned unpleasantly. "I left him back in the barn. It was on fire when I left. I don't think he'll cause us any problems."

Grundy nodded shortly. "What do you want us to do?"

"I want to save my ranch here. We can get us another marshal," Capwell said, looking at Grundy in a new light. "Say, maybe you'd like the job. I'll bet you'd be a good lawman."

Grundy appeared to think about it for a minute, then smiled and said, "I believe I like that idea."

"What about me?" Slim said.

Capwell had fully expected to turn Slim in as one of the rustlers, but things had changed in his favor and he was feeling generous. "Why, you can be the deputy."

Slim grinned and bobbed his head at the thought.

Capwell brought them back to reality. "Mount up, gentlemen. The first order of business is," he got on the marshal's horse and continued, "we're going to have a little necktie party."

Grundy and Slim remounted their horses and the three men rode as fast as they could toward Rattlesnake.

CHAPTER 24

GIMPY Higgins was snoring, but Mattie didn't mind. At least he didn't want to talk. She was tired of talking and even more tired of thinking. She just wanted all of this to be over. Mattie tried to convince herself that the last few months had been nothing more than a bad dream. She closed her eyes, hoping that when she opened them she'd be back in her bed and Joe would be sleeping beside her. But when she opened them, she was still in jail and Joe was still dead.

She heard horses outside. Marshal Cobb must have returned. Gimpy snorted and moved around, shifting the shotgun from one knee to the other.

The office door opened and three sets of boots stomped in. She felt a sense of relief. Marshal Cobb must have brought in Luther Capwell and Chester Grundy. The door to the jail opened and in walked Capwell, followed by Grundy, followed by . . . Slim?

Mattie called to him. "Slim, how in the world . . . ?"

But wait. Why did Capwell have the jail keys? He opened Mattie's cell. Gimpy woke up, fuzzy from his nap.

"What in tarnation?" Gimpy didn't get anything more out before Grundy knocked him across the side of the head with the back of his pistol. Mattie winced at the sound of metal hitting flesh and bone. Gimpy slumped to the floor, his shotgun resting by his side.

"Come on, Mrs. Quinn." Capwell stood there holding his hand out, waiting for her to meekly take it.

"Stay away from me, all of you." Mattie pressed herself against the cell wall.

"Come now, Mrs. Quinn." Capwell frowned slightly. "You're not going to cause us trouble, are you?"

"What are you doing here?" she asked, hoping her fright wasn't evident. "Where's Marshal Cobb and Jefferson Birch?"

Capwell shook his head in mock sorrow. "It's a shame about them. Birch is back on my land trying to put out a fire and the marshal lent me his horse."

She looked from one face to the other, finally resting on her former ranch hand. "Slim, what's this all about?"

Slim smiled and said, "Why, Mrs. Quinn. We're getting you out of jail."

Capwell extended a hand again and said, "Come with us. We'll escort you outside."

She looked over at Gimpy, who had slumped to the floor. A nasty bruise was already forming where Grundy had pistol-whipped him. Reluctantly, she accompanied them out of the jailhouse.

When they got to the door, Mattie looked up at the stars. One of the men hit her on the back of the head. She reached up to touch the lump, and the stars began to spin in circles in the night sky. They winked once and then they all went out.

CHAPTER 25

BIRCH rode fast. He knew where Capwell was headed and he had to stop him. He'd hoped to catch up to him on the road into town, but instead Birch found the marshal in the middle of the road lying in a pool of blood. Cobb was near death.

Birch stopped and examined Cobb's wound. It was a single shot to the chest.

Gasping for breath, Cobb said, "Got away . . ." He coughed up some blood, then continued, his breathing heavy. "Capwell . . . Mattie Quinn . . . hanging . . . "

Birch started to move the pain-wracked lawman, but Cobb protested. "Go . . . I'm fine . . . "

Birch nodded. "Try to hang on. After this is over, I'll get . . ." There was no need to finish his sentence. Gordy Cobb was dead.

By the time he reached the edge of town, Birch was hoping he'd catch them breaking Mattie Quinn out of jail. But the office door stood open. He heard groaning inside and found an old man with a shotgun, nursing a bruised temple. A trickle of blood oozed from his head wound. The white-whiskered fellow caught sight of Birch and raised his shotgun.

"You the feller who pistol-whupped me?"

Birch replied, "No, I'm not, but I can lead you to the fellow who did. Luther Capwell killed the marshal outside of town and I have to go after him. I could use your help."

The old man narrowed his eyes and said, "They took that young widow woman, too. Let's go."

Birch asked, "Did Capwell say where he was taking her?"

The old man rubbed his whiskers in thought, wincing a little every time he ran across the bruise. "I was out cold at the time, but I'd bet they didn't want to run into you again."

Birch and his companion left the jailhouse. Birch got down on one knee and peered at the street. Several horses had left town, heading north. They mounted their horses and followed the trail, Birch reading the sparse signs and hoping he was right.

Five minutes out of town, the tracks veered off the trail to the right. Gimpy grunted and said, "This path leads to an abandoned ranch. I think it's part of Capwell's property now."

That made sense to Birch and they continued on with growing determination. Soon they were in sight of a small house and beyond it, they saw a couple of figures throwing a rope over a high post. Birch guessed that they were Grundy and Slim. Another man, Capwell, stood nearby with the limp figure of a woman in his arms.

Birch withdrew his gun and fired a warning shot, then spurred Cactus into a gallop. Grundy and Slim returned the gunfire. Capwell laid Mattie Quinn out on the ground.

Gimpy took up residence behind a water trough and took pot shots in the dark.

"Give it up, Capwell," Birch shouted. "You're surrounded."

Capwell laughed in response, then shouted back, "By you and that old man?" He fired at Birch.

Birch was able to take cover behind an old cottonwood tree. He could still see most of the action, but he couldn't see Mattie Quinn. Gimpy fired at a slender figure trying to run from behind the split-rail fence to the back of a shed. A yelp of pain told Birch that the old man hit his mark.

Birch took in the lay of the land. He wanted to circle around and find Mattie Quinn. When he was just about ready to start, he turned around to find Slim holding a gun on him. His left arm hung useless by his side, courtesy of Gimpy. The sleeve was stained dark with blood.

"Hold it, Birch," the young cowhand said. "I've got you covered. Drop your gun."

Birch dropped his weapon and said, "Why are you doing this, Slim? You know they're just going to use you and kill you when they get a chance."

Slim smiled and shook his head slowly. "It won't work, Birch. Mr. Capwell has been good to me. He'll take care of me."

"So you'll even hang a woman to get what you want?"

Slim frowned briefly. "I don't like the idea of hanging a woman, but Mr. Capwell says we have to do this to clear ourselves."

Birch noticed that Slim was swaying slightly. His face had gone pasty from the lack of blood. Birch got ready to tackle Slim at the right moment, but the former Quinn ranch hand suddenly frowned.

"I know what you're thinking, Birch," Slim said, cocking back the hammer on his gun. "You think you can take me when I pass out. But I won't give you that chance. You'll be dead before I get that weak."

Birch looked beyond Slim and said, "There's someone right behind you, Slim. You may as well drop your gun."

Slim shook his head and replied confidently, "You're bluffing again. I've already told you it won't work. When will you give it up?"

A voice in the darkness behind Slim said, "This time he's right, Slim. Drop your gun."

"Omaha," Slim said and turned, his gun still in his hand.

Omaha fired and Slim dropped to the ground. Birch picked up his gun and nodded to Omaha, who had his left arm in a sling.

Omaha looked down at Slim's body. "I liked Slim, but I guess he just got too greedy."

Birch put his hand on Omaha's right shoulder and said, "A lot of people in this town got too greedy."

Omaha asked, "Where's Mattie?"

Birch noticed that it was the first time Omaha hadn't tried to correct himself and call her "Mrs. Quinn."

"She's over by the corral entrance. Grundy and Capwell still have to be dealt with," Birch said. "I'll go after Grundy." Omaha nodded and they split up, circling around the corral while Gimpy kept the two outlaws busy with his shotgun.

Grundy was hiding behind the corner of a shed. Birch was planning on sneaking up on him, but Grundy must have sensed that the former Texas Ranger was behind him because he turned and fired. Birch took a dive and rolled, then aimed and shot.

The shot forced Grundy back against the shed, clutching his side. As Birch was getting up, Grundy fired again, grazing Birch's cheek. Birch dropped to all fours and started crawling toward Grundy and made a grab for his ankles. Grundy staggered away from him and kicked Birch in the shoulder, forcing the ex-Ranger to drop his gun.

Birch grabbed Grundy's boot and pulled, sending his attacker to the ground. Grundy tried to get off another shot, but Birch knocked the gun out of his hand and they scrambled in the dirt for the gun closest to them.

Grundy's hand closed around the gun and he pointed it at Birch, ready to shoot. Another shot rang out and Grundy fell over, dead. Mattie was on her knees, both hands wrapped around the handle of the other gun. She fell forward, hard to the ground.

Birch got up and limped over to her, gently removing the gun from her clutch. Omaha was by her side, shooting Birch a look that told him to back off.

Gimpy approached with his prisoner, Luther Capwell, hands tied behind his back.

"When my family finds out about this," Capwell sneered, "they'll send for me. My father is rich."

"Who said anything about putting you in jail?" Gimpy said, picking up the noose and dangling it in front of Capwell.

The fallen cattle baron's face turned white and he sputtered, "You can't do that to me. I have rights. You wouldn't dare . . ."

Omaha couldn't keep still any longer. "But you were willing to hang an innocent woman, weren't you?"

Capwell began to beg. "I can pay you. I have lots of money."

Birch held up the satchel and said, "You mean this?"

That silenced Luther Capwell. He stood there, shaking.

Birch looked over at Omaha and Mattie and was suddenly very weary and very sad. The widow Quinn was leaning against Omaha for support. She touched her head and winced.

Gimpy said, "Well, come on. What are we waiting for? Let's string up this fellow." He poked Capwell with his shotgun.

Capwell said to Birch, "You can't let them do this. You're kind of a lawman."

Birch shook his head and said, "I'm not the law here and you just killed the only lawman in Rattlesnake." Birch had promised himself he'd never see another innocent man hang from the limb of a tree, but Luther Capwell was far from innocent.

Turning to Gimpy, Omaha, and Mattie Quinn, Birch said, "If he was in my custody, I'd have to take him to jail, but you do what you think is right."

With that, Birch mounted Cactus and rode off.

The next morning, Birch rode out to the Quinn ranch to gather his things and to say his goodbyes. He'd helped the doctor bring back the marshal's body and had spent the rest of the night at the jail. Then Gimpy took over and Birch left.

It was fairly late in the morning and he hadn't expected anyone to be at the main house when he arrived. But the events of last night had taken their toll and both Omaha and Mattie Quinn were just sitting down to breakfast.

She wore her blue dress and insisted on cooking Birch's breakfast. He took pleasure in watching her bustle around the kitchen, breaking eggs into the cast iron fry pan, and cutting thick slices of fresh-baked bread.

"Now you just go sit yourself down at the table, Jefferson Birch," she said with a smile. "The least I can do is cook you a hearty meal for your trip." She flipped the eggs over and stepped back as they hissed in the hot grease.

"Birch?" Her smile had been replaced by a solemn look.

"Yes?"

"You know, you can stay here if you like." Mattie Quinn looked down and blushed. "I mean, if you don't have any place to go right now." She looked at him.

"Thank you, Mrs. Quinn."

"My name is Mattie," she said softly.

"I have to go. I got a telegram yesterday from my employer," he lied. It was for the best. Omaha was there for her. "I have to meet him in Helena for another job."

"Oh," was all she said, turning quickly away to put the fried eggs on a plate.

As he headed for the table, she added, "Well, if you change your mind, I'll still be here."

He paused and said, "Thanks," without turning around.

Omaha was sitting at the table already. He watched Birch warily.

Omaha grunted, "I ought to thank you for saving my life and Mattie's as well. If you hadn't stuck around, she'd be dead and Capwell would have the ranch. By the way, was it him who ordered Grundy to kill Blackiston and Mr. Quinn?"

Birch explained, "Blackiston ordered Grundy to kill Joe Quinn, thinking that a helpless widow would sell her ranch fast and move away. But Mrs. Quinn surprised him by staying. He tried to scare her off her land, but that didn't work, either."

"Instead, she hired you," Omaha replied.

Birch nodded. "Chester Grundy reported to Capwell every move Blackiston made. When Blackiston ordered Grundy to kill Joe Quinn, Capwell thought it would be a good opportunity to kill Blackiston, framing Mattie Quinn for the murder. After all, the widow never made any secret that she believed Blackiston was behind her husband's death. Then Capwell could step in and take over all of Blackiston's property. It would have made him even wealthier and more powerful."

"So why did Capwell steal the horses?"

Birch answered, "When Mattie wasn't taken in for suspicion of Blackiston's murder, Capwell started the rumor that she was a rustler."

"I was ready to kill him with my bare hands when I heard that he'd started it," Omaha added.

Birch continued. "When Capwell reported his horses gone and the marshal didn't do anything about it, he had Blackiston's horses stolen, thinking that would stir the town to act. After all, only a low-down skunk would steal a dead man's horses. But no one seemed concerned."

Omaha laughed. "Capwell forgot how much everyone hated Blackiston. No one would care that his horses were stolen, even after he was dead." The ranch hand grew serious and continued, "So Capwell arranged with Slim to find his own stolen horses on Quinn land."

Birch nodded and said, "He was too greedy to use Blackiston's horses. He wanted to keep them. And when Mattie had been put away, he also had the Collins horses stolen to make the townsfolk turn against her."

"But how did he expect anyone to think she'd had anything to do with the rustled Collins horses when she was in jail?"

Birch smiled and replied, "It didn't matter. The townspeople were supposed to become so angry over the loss of a small rancher's horses that they would string up the nearest available accused rustler—Mattie Quinn." He added, "It was also supposed to point the finger at you, me, Charley, and Slim as members of Mattie's gang of rustlers."

"Slim, too?" Omaha raised his eyebrows in surprise.

"Capwell was just using Slim. I tried to tell him, but he wouldn't listen to me."

Omaha shook his head.

Birch added, "What will you do about the cattle drive? You don't have enough hands."

Mattie came in with a plate filled with flapjacks, eggs, and steak. She'd overheard Birch's question because she responded, "We can always use an extra hand for the drive. Are you interested, Mr. Birch?"

"Thanks for the offer, but I'm heading in a different direction. I have to report to Arthur Tisdale."

She smiled and said, "That's all right. We'll be talking to the Collins family today. Most likely they'll accompany us on the drive, especially now that we've found their horses."

After the meal, Birch packed his things and saddled up Cactus.

"Are you certain you can't stay, Mr. Birch?" Mattie asked.

Omaha caught Birch's eye.

"I really have to go." Birch patted his shirt pocket to emphasize the nonexistent telegram. He felt something hard—it was his Tisdale Investigation badge.

Both Omaha and Mattie raised their arms and waved as Birch mounted Cactus.

Where he was going, he had no idea; but when he got there, he'd wire Arthur Tisdale. Then he'd find a hotel, take a hot bath, and buy a bottle of good whiskey to ease his aching muscles.

Tipping his hat toward Mattie Quinn and Omaha, Birch pointed Cactus west toward Helena and rode away.

If you have enjoyed this book and would like to receive details of other Walker Western titles, please write to:

Western Editor
Walker and Company
720 Fifth Avenue
New York, NY 10019